Desert of Darkness

Desert of Darkness
by Ruth Wissmann

A CORONET BOOK
published by

GROSSET & DUNLAP
A NATIONAL GENERAL COMPANY
Publishers   New York

Desert of Darkness

1

AHEAD OF THEM lay the arid world of the desert. Here cactus grew, and tumbleweeds like spheres of golden filigree, rolled helplessly before a tyrant wind. The scene was tinted blue and lavender and taupe where jutting rocks and Joshua trees cast their shadows across the rippled sand. These trees, these tall gray-green outgrowths of the earth, reached in all directions with thorny arms as they forever sought the unattainable. And she shivered.

"It's a strangely awesome place," she said.

"Restful," he told her.

The engine purred as the car carried them over a twisting road that he drove cautiously, but not without his ever present self-assurance. She knew, however, that thoughts churned his mind, for there had been miles when he had been as quiet as these bleak, ominous surroundings through which they traveled. From her face dropped the mask of serenity that she usually wore, revealing a frown of apprehension. There was no denying this sense of forboding that had haunted her this day, riding with them like an unseen, unwelcome passenger. Had he, too, been aware of it: this uneasiness that seemed to hold her fast?

"What's wrong?" he asked. "You act as though you're frightened."

"Perhaps I am. I wish we hadn't come here."

"Vickie! What's the matter? Usually you want to accompany me on these business trips and fret when I can't take you along."

"I know," she said, detecting the rough edge of irritation in his voice, and her eyes turned again to the gathering gloom. Night falls swiftly on the desert, and she wondered if they would arrive at their destination before darkness.

As always when she felt fearful and insecure, she fingered the glowing hair with which nature had endowed her, twisting a long strand of its reddish gold around her finger. This mane reaching her shoulders was, she felt, her only claim to beauty. However, its very vividness was what paled her face by comparison and gave it a kind of anonymity; her features were regular and small as was her slender figure.

"It must be the desolation that bothers you," her husband was saying, "or do you suffer from agoraphobia?"

"Fortunately not," she replied, "and it isn't only the desolation and remoteness of this region, it's—savage and—eerie somehow."

He laughed. "Come on, you're too imaginative and nervous. When we reach Burant's house and have cocktails, you'll be all right again."

She nodded, but did not agree. "How long do you think it will take?" she asked.

"What? Oh, you mean persuading James Burant to sell that property in Palm Springs? Who can say? Perhaps we can clear the way this weekend, but then it might not be that easy. Lecursi really wants to buy, but if Burant is not especially eager to sell. . . . " He shrugged.

"Phil, I can't help but wonder why this man lives in such an isolated spot. How lonely he must be out here!"

"Lecursi told me he has a comfortable home, and until his wife died, he wasn't alone."

"When did that happen?"

"Five—six months ago, I think."

Vickie almost asked if the woman had died of sheer loneliness, but instead she said nothing, and the narrow road, traced in sand, carried them on and on until at last, off in the blue and gloomy distance, she saw yucca and ocotilla surrounding a brown adobe house with a roof of red tile; a rambling kind of dwelling that seemed synonymous with Old Mexico.

"There it is," Phil said, "our journey's end."

"Mmmm," she murmured, peering into the haze of the early evening. "I see it, but in this light there is something almost unreal about the scene, wouldn't you say?"

"It looks real enough to me and quite inviting."

It was a painting done in soft shades of violet, blue and rose, and she was in it and disturbed, for around her was this suffocating monster of premonition, this godawful feeling of doom. A drink might help, she told herself with determination, and the house will be cheerful and our stay within it pleasant. Hovering in the back of her mind was the thought that she must see her doctor. Obviously she was in need of something for her nerves. Premonitions were not strangers to Vickie. She had known these moments before, but never, never had the ominous feeling been so persistent, so gripping; never before had it been a thing she could not banish by turning her thoughts into other channels.

As they neared the house she noticed how attractive it was; inviting and colorful. Shutters of red-orange contrasted excitedly with the soft brown of the walls. How foolish she had been, permitting her thoughts to bedevil her about coming here! There was nothing cold or forbidding about this place at all. She must try to control her emotions, attempt to curb her inane fears.

With a growing interest she looked at the mailbox mounted on a wooden wheel, weathered and gray, that stood alongside the adobe wall near the road. Here was a gate of wrought iron carrying the name, "Flor de Desierto." Appropriate, she told herself. The house is indeed a desert flower. She breathed deeply. Yes, this was better. These were the thoughts that should fill her mind.

"Lovely," she said, and he smiled.

"Do you feel better now?"

"Yes," she told him, although it was not true.

He pulled to a stop, stepped from the car, and she moved into the driver's seat and watched as he unlatched the gates that swung slowly open to admit them. She drove through, as they seemed to be waiting for her to do, then slipped back to the passenger side. Now she listened as he closed the latch with a firm, metallic sound of finality. A hated, unwelcome thought wormed its way back into her mind. Would these gates ever open for her again? And she was angered. Why do I permit such ideas to enter my head? I'm a fool. I really am.

Now he was back inside the car, and they rolled along a driveway toward the entrance of the house. She looked at the heavily carved door, and then at him. "Do you love me?" she asked suddenly.

He turned and looked at her, his lips parted, his eyes wide in surprise. "Whatever made you ask that, Vickie?" he said. "You are in a state! We've been married for five years, and I've loved you every minute of them—well, except that day you tore down a fence with our new car thirty minutes after driving it away from the dealer's. I'll admit there was a moment or two then when. . . . " He laughed, reached over and caressed her cheek. "Let's go in, shall we?"

As they stepped from the car the wind met them with a rush of tiny, sharp grains of sand stinging their faces and trying to enter their eyes, noses and mouths. They ran toward the recessed door that was opening and revealing a girl with black hair and a complexion honeyed by the desert sun.

"How do you do? Are you the Bishops?" she asked with traces of a Spanish accent.

"We are," Phil replied, brushing at his coat and windblown hair.

"Come in. Mr. Corbett is expecting you."

A tall slender man came forward, his hand extended. "I'm Norman Corbett," he said, "Jim Burant's brother-in-law."

"Happy to meet you. I'm Phil Bishop, and this is my wife, Vickie."

"You've had a long drive," the man said. "Did you have difficulty finding the house?"

"None," Phil replied, "but I had explicit directions."

"And they're a necessity," Norman Corbett declared. "Jim drove to Palm Springs this morning and hasn't returned yet. He should be along shortly, however. Would you like a cocktail?"

"You have no idea how much," Vickie heard her husband say as she studied, with the eyes of a professional decorator, the large room into which they were being led. The furniture was sturdy and masculine, giving an air of stability and permanence to the room.

"This is enchanting," she remarked.

"I suppose it is," Norman said, smiling at her, reminding her of Gregory Peck. "My sister Kathleen always like it very much."

"What would you like? A martini? A margarita?"

"I'd like a margarita," Vickie said. "It's been a long time since I've had one."

"The same," Phil said, and they sat down in the deep, comfortable chairs that the man indicated and watched as he opened double doors along the wall that revealed a modern bar. It had a jarring, incongruous appearance in this room of old Spanish charm.

The dark-haired girl who had admitted them entered with ice. Her colorful blouse and full ruffled skirt fit into the scene with perfection, too much perfection. For a moment that sense of unreality that Vickie had felt before flared up. The house, the room, the girl, her clothes. A stage. A play.

"This is Anita, and she will be most happy to be of service to you at any time," they were told. "She and her mother have been taking care of this house for nearly a year."

"Do you have enough salt for the glasses, Mr. Corbett?" the girl asked quietly.

"Yes, Anita. Thank you."

With a nod she left the room, but not before examining Vickie's apparel, face and hair. Vickie, too, stared at the young woman. It was not her colorful clothing or the shining hair caught in a ribbon at the nape of her neck that Vickie noticed, it was the expression in those dark eyes. What did she read there? Caution? Distrust? Or was it fear?

The cocktails were delicious and potent. Vickie sipped hers slowly and said little while listening to the men search for a subject of mutual interest to discuss. Their efforts were rather embarrassingly unsuccessful, and Vickie, lulled by the alcohol leaned back and contemplated the house and its occupants. While there was nothing tangible on which she could base her impression, a coldness, a malevolence was present that was out of character in this house. The disturbing undercurrent of discord hung like shadows around them, and was something the room could not conceal.

Later Vickie and Phil were led upstairs and along a balcony extending in a U around the flagstone patio below. The room they were to occupy, Vickie found, opened from here, and in the outer wall was a wide window framing an impressive scene of miles and miles of desert sand.

After they were alone, Phil smiled at her. "You didn't expect our destination to be quite like this, did you? What an attractive place this is! My client didn't do it justice with his description. See, your fretting was a waste of time and energy as usual. Feel better now?"

She ignored his last question and began to unpack. "It is an interesting house," she said. "You're right. It isn't at all what I expected."

"I don't particularly care for this Corbett, though," he continued. "He's okay, I suppose, but—aloof. Notice that?"

"No, I wasn't aware of it."

"Well, I was. He's hard to talk to. Uncommunicative. I always feel uncomfortable around someone like him; I wouldn't trust him. Do you know what I mean? No one ever knows what's going on inside his head, and as a rule it's nothing good. I don't like this kind of person."

"Then it's fortunate that your business isn't with him."

"It is a break," he declared just as a knock was heard at their door.

Vickie opened it to find an older woman there, attractive and smiling.

"I am Mrs. Pomares," she said. "May I be of any help?"

Vickie smiled at her. "Thank you, but I think not," she replied. "We have little to unpack, and everything is fine." The woman nodded at both of them and left. Then Vickie turned toward her husband. "I have to admit," she said, "that we are being made to feel welcome." He looked at her with an, "I told you so" expression on his face.

Now Vickie glanced up from her cosmetic case and listened. There was the sound of an approaching car followed by a short, sharp squeal of brakes. "Apparently our host has returned," she said. "I suppose he went to Palm Springs to reach a decision regarding the sale of his property there."

"And let's hope this decision is an affirmative one," Phil answered. "It will bring us a nice fee."

After showering, Vickie selected an emerald-green dress to wear, because it did fantastic things for her eyes and was a natural complement for her hair. She added a gold chain necklace, coral lipstick and soft green eyeshadow. Looking into the mirror she was not unhappy at what she saw. Would Phil offer a word of approval? But no, he seldom did, and silently they returned to the living room.

Their host was in his thirties: genial, tall, muscular, with the complexion of one who had spent many hours outdoors. His hair was nearly as dark as Anita's, and his brown eyes lingered on Vickie. She hoped Phil might show a spark of jealousy. He didn't, but then he never had.

Now there were more cocktails, but no discussion of the

prospective sale that had brought these people together. Vickie knew that this was not the time, not yet. This was the warming period, the pretense of being drawn closely together by mutual admiration and friendship. The softening up, the breaking down, the well-concealed studying of each other's potentialities. This was the game, the one called Buyer and Seller. By devious routes of circles and mazes, the two players might finally come together at the square marked Home. One might win. One might lose. Quite often it would be a draw.

Anita appeared and announced dinner. Vickie did not miss the guarded look that passed between this girl and her employer. Nor did she miss seeing Norman Corbett witness it. At the table Vickie compared the two men. Jim Burant lacked a certain refinement that Norman Corbett possessed. The former was friendlier, warmer, an earthy type of individual. His manner was jovial, his laughter louder. Norman seemed to be one of those who are watchers of people, who listened more than he spoke as he observed with secret thoughts those around him. What had drawn these two men together? The woman Kathleen, who had been wife to one and sister to the other? Were they friends? She doubted it.

The dinner was delicious, the wine rich and soothing, and the dining room spacious. Along one wall rose a massive candelabra, a fireplace nearly filled the end of the room, and in the outer wall were two large windows, heavily draped. They were at Vickie's back which made her uncomfortable. It was a senseless thing she knew, this uneasiness caused by being seated with the windows behind her, this feeling that from there she was being watched, but it remained with her.

"Are you chilly, Mrs. Bishop?" their host asked, seeing, or perhaps sensing her discomfort.

"Oh, no. Not at all."

"She's Vickie. Call her Vickie," her husband said, "and me Phil."

This was his jolly-good-fellow role, Vickie told herself; a part Phil enjoyed so much he overplayed it at times.

"Thank you, and call me Jim." The man's eyes turned toward her. "Okay, Vickie?"

"Yes, Jim," she said and smiled, for this was her role in the drama being performed. She had played it many times and knew the script well.

"Vickie, Phil, Norman, Jim," their host said while his eyes lingered on her. "Okay?"

"Okay, Jim," she replied, returning his steady gaze.

"I like the way you say that," he told her. "Your voice is soft and sweet."

"Thank you," she murmured and a moment later glanced toward her husband. The smile on his face revealed his pleasure with her, the progress she was making with his prospective buyer. A gnawing bleak kind of emptiness crept over her.

Anita filled their wine glasses again, while the candles cast flickering lights on the five occupants of the room. In their dancing rays, Vickie's eyes were drawn to Norman because he was watching her. She found his gaze speculative, and tried to read the thoughts lying behind it. What was his part in this production? Perhaps he played no role. Perhaps he was the solemn audience. She hoped he would not leave before the play was over, for he seemed to be a kind of stabilizer, this quiet man who sat and watched. She thought he might even be able to act as prompter. Like herself, she sensed that he, too, had seen this drama before.

When dinner was over, Phil and Vickie returned to their room. "What do you think?" she asked.

"It's too early to tell," he said, his blue eyes glowing and a wisp of his sandy hair hanging between them. We made progress tonight—especially you, Vickie. He likes you. He's a friendly, likable fellow, isn't he?"

"Yes," she said without his enthusiasm. Why don't you care? she wanted to ask. Why are you so pragmatic? Even if he made love to me, I wonder if you would object. Probably not. She undressed and lay down on the bed, and watched him as he prepared to retire. How ambitious he was! How quick and decisive his actions were! Never did he waste a moment, nor an opportunity. A man with a purpose. She closed her eyes.

Some time later she stirred in her sleep and into her consciousness crept the sound of voices seemingly coming from far away. She tried to shut them out, these meaningless noises, disturbing her slumber and causing a feeling of distress within her. The sounds persisted and finally succeeded in waking her, and she lay quite still listening. Somewhere a feminine voice was speaking, but in tones too low to be audible. The reply was that of a man, one who had spoken with annoyance and impatience.

With her curiosity aroused, Vickie sat up in bed and strained to hear what must be an argument. However the words were fading, receding, apparently from the patio to the interior of the house. After a moment all was silent again. She eased herself from the bed and quietly crossed the floor, pulled back the draperies a little, and looked out at the night. The Joshua trees appeared grotesque in the moonlight that colored the sand silver and blue. Shivering she returned to bed, but some time passed before she could sleep again.

During this interval she stared into the darkness and wondered about the occupants of this house. Had she overheard a lovers' quarrel? Anita and—Norman? Jim? She thought of how few times she and Phil had quarreled, but then—were they truly lovers? Here was a question she had often pondered during the five years of their marriage.

How emotionally exhausting their wedded years had been! Never had she known her real place in Phil's heart. Never had she been able to break through the wall he had built so strongly around himself, this barricade that concealed the true feelings of Philip Bishop.

Her eyes turned to the pillow next to hers where his head lay unmoving and his breath could be heard in the slow ebbing and flowing of deep sleep. They had met, and in such a short time they had married. How attracted they had been to each other! Strangers in love. Now what? What did the future hold?

Then in her mind she saw Norman Corbett. Quiet, composed, remote. As he had observed them this evening, how had he felt? Did he laugh at them? Despise them or what? She sighed and closed her eyes with drowsiness, too weary, too puzzled to seek the answers.

The following morning Vickie was roused by the dazzling daylight thrusting itself through the drawn draperies and found, to her surprise, that she was alone. Her wristwatch revealed that it was half past eight. Phil was always up by seven. She wondered why he had not awakened her.

She left the bed and opened the curtains to look at the desert scene of this bright morning. While the moon had painted it silver, the sun had restored it to its real color and the sky was blue, clear and tranquil.

The silence of this place made her conscious of the very air pressing against her eardrums. And her heart—was its beating audible? She could feel herself breathing with the same tenseness that gripped her yesterday, and looking at the vast space beyond the window, she wondered how it would be to find oneself out there—lost and alone. She shuddered, and quickly turned her thoughts away from the picture, seeing instead the buildings, the hills, the people, the misty air of home—San Francisco.

As she dressed, she could not quiet the irritation stirring within her because Phil had left the room while she still

slept. Even though she knew this feeling was unreasonable, it was there. She pulled on a yellow woolen dress,
threw a soft orange sweater across her shoulders and
stepped out onto the balcony. From here she looked down
at the patio, pausing to admire the flagstone, the potted
palms, and the well with decorative wrought iron arching
across it holding a pulley and bucket.

After a moment she walked toward the main section of
the house and descended the stairs to the large center hall.
To her right was the living room, and to the left the dining
room. "Anita?" she called hesitantly. How quiet it was!
Why did she not hear the sound of men's voices? The
house was as still as the eternal desert surrounding it.

Swiftly she crossed the dining room and opened the
door through which dinner had been served the night
before. The kitchen was large with brick walls and tiled
floors. In the center of the room was a table circled with
eight chairs. The aroma of coffee filled the air and three
used cups remained on the table.

"Oh, Mrs. Bishop!" a voice said, and Vickie turned to
find Anita standing at a door on the far side of the room.
"Good morning."

"Good morning," Vickie replied. "I've been trying to find
my husband."

"He is not here. No one is, but you and me. I'll pour
some coffee for you and get your breakfast now. My mother has—"

"He isn't here?" Vickie asked. "I don't understand."

"He went with Mr. Burant to Palm Springs, and Mr.
Corbett has driven my mother to Los Angeles to be with
her sister who became ill during the night."

Vickie looked at the girl, with the feeling that she might
be lying. "I'm sorry about your aunt," she said.

"Thank you. A neighbor of hers called here. It was early
this morning, five o'clock, perhaps."

"I see. And what time did my husband leave?"

"Seven-thirty, I think. Would you like some eggs? And we have sweet rolls that my mother baked yesterday."

"Just a roll and coffee please." In the light pouring through the window near the sink, Vickie could see tell-tale puffs beneath the girl's eyes; the evidence that she had cried during the night. Her age, Vickie judged, was probably nineteen or twenty. She was a rounded, full-blown kind of girl who would always have to battle extra poundage. "Do you like living here, Anita?" she asked, as she pulled out a chair and sat down at the table.

There was a moment before the girl replied. Then, "Yes," she said, and her hand paused before pouring coffee into the cup for Vickie. "But it is so quiet and kind of—scary."

"I agree," Vickie said. "It is that. When will Mr. Burant and my husband return? Did they say?"

"No, they didn't."

Vickie sipped the strong brew and tried to quell the anger smouldering within her. Phil should have wakened her, taken her with him. She had never seen Palm Springs. "I must have slept quite soundly," she said, "although I do recall waking during the night. I don't know what time it was, however."

"It is difficult to sleep in this house," Anita said. "Mrs. Bishop, may I sit here and have coffee with you?"

"Of course. Please do. Tell me, why isn't it easy to sleep in a place as quiet as this?"

Anita's cup was almost to her lips, but she replaced it into the saucer and then said, "The night is not always quiet."

"Oh?"

"Sometimes there is the sound of a voice calling," the girl said in a hushed tone.

"A voice? That's what wakened me during the night. Two voices, however," and Vickie saw a flush appear in the girl's cheeks, and regretted her words.

"I'm sorry you were disturbed. It was Mr. Burant and I. We had a disagreement."

"It was nothing," Vickie said. "I fell asleep again almost immediately."

"He does not always believe what I say—what I know is true."

Vickie looked up to find anguish in the girl's dark eyes. She was surprised and embarrassed that Anita was confiding in her this way. How badly she must need companionship. "Do you want to tell me what's worrying you?" she asked.

A dark and potent shadow seemed to reach across the table and touch Vickie with fingers of ice. "Perhaps I can help you," she said, feeling a shiver along her spine. The blind leading the blind, she thought.

The girl shook her head. "No one can. It is this house, something that remains here."

I am right, Vickie thought. The venomous atmosphere was not—is not of my imagination. "Something? What do you mean?"

"I—I cannot say."

"I'll tell you how I feel," Vickie said. "I'm glad you didn't leave this morning with the others. I should hate to be left alone in here."

Now a cautious expression veiled the girl's face. Had their moment of trust and closeness vanished? Apparently it had. Anita was withdrawing. "It is remote here," she said quietly. "We are far from others."

Vickie nodded. "I'm not accustomed to this kind of living," she stated, knowing she was beginning to tread on forbidden ground. How angry Phil would be if he could hear her say anything uncomplimentary about this house! "That's what I meant," she said, "about not wanting to be here alone. Actually it's a beautiful place."

"You are from a city, yes?"

"San Francisco."

Anita nodded. "No, you would never be happy. You could not live here." She offered the plate of rolls to Vickie. "Would you like another?"

"Thank you. I can't resist. Your mother is an excellent cook."

"She enjoys doing it." The girl looked thoughtfully at Vickie, and after a moment she said, "You are beautiful. I saw how Mr. Burant and Mr. Corbett looked at you last night."

"Oh. No, I'm not, but thank you for saying so anyway."

"She looks very much like you. Her eyes are green like yours, but her hair is more blond—I mean less red."

"Who?" Vickie asked, perplexed.

"Why, Kathleen, of course."

"Kathleen?"

"Yes. Jim's wife, Kathleen Burant."

Vickie stared at the girl in astonishment. Now, suddenly, Mr. Burant was Jim and his wife was being referred to as if she still lived! This girl, somehow, had muffed her lines.

"But—I must have been misinformed. I understood Mrs. Burant was dead," Vickie said uncertainly.

"Yes," the girl said firmly. "I must remember that. She is dead. She is dead."

"Oh, God!" Vickie murmured, and saw Anita's eyes look intently around them, and then stare over Vickie's right shoulder. Frozen with horror, Vickie sat immobilized for a long and agonizing moment before she could find the courage to force herself to turn to see that no one was there. *The girl is demented. She is mad.*

"Kathleen hates me," the girl added.

Vickie could scarcely breathe as she searched for words to speak, feeling herself hopelessly inadequate to meet this turn of events. *I must humor her,* she thought. *Alone here* with this strange girl, I must say nothing that might disturb her more.

"Anita, I'm sure she doesn't hate you. You're very sweet. No one could dislike you."

The dark eyes widened. "She does. She does. You do not know. She blames me for what happened to her," she added in a whisper.

"No, Anita. I'm sure she doesn't blame you."

How did the woman die? Vickie wanted to ask. What has been taking place in this house?

"She will kill me!" Anita cried out in a voice filled with terror. "I know this. She will kill me, and there is no way I can stop her."

Suddenly Anita was on her feet, overturning her cup as she rose, and with a cry, ran from the room. Vickie sat as one turned to stone, her eyes on the coffee spreading across the colorful design of the table before her.

Some time passed before she gathered the dishes together and rinsed them in the sink. Then, after sponging away all traces of the spilled liquid, she returned to the center hall. She looked at the graceful curve of the stairway and its bannister of black wrought iron. Then her eyes went to the living room, and hesitantly she entered it. How different it appeared from the way it was last night! The very atmosphere had altered.

Her gaze traveled up the walls and to the beamed ceiling far above in this room that was one and a half stories high. All the cheeriness and warmth of last night was now gone, and a gray haze seemed to hang in shadows around her. The perfume of burning wood from the fireplace was now reduced to the aridness of ashes. She walked toward the windows; she would open the draperies to let the sun pour in and wash away the dreariness that was here. But as she crossed the room, she paused and pulled her sweater closer to her. How cold it was! There was something almost uncanny about the frigid chill that slowly wrapped itself around her.

"Oh, God," she murmured, knowing it would take more than sunshine to dispel the iciness present in this room. Then she spun around suddenly while her heart hammered against her breast. She had seen a movement of some kind, hadn't she? A swaying kind of a—wisp of smoke? But there was nothing here. Everything was still, so very still. It must have been the play of light as it seeped through the fibers of the drapes. Yes, of course that was it. Anita had unnerved her. That sudden unexpected outburst, those declarations of the girl's deranged mind had perturbed her more than she had thought.

Walking toward the hall, she knew she should be running. She wanted to run, but then if she moved slowly, inconspicuously, she might be safe from—from what? When she reached the hallway, she turned, looked back and caught her breath. The distortion was there for only a split second, this seeing the room as if through the wrong end of binoculars, but it had turned her blood to ice water. Now she was running along the hall and up the stairs as swiftly as a blast of wind sweeping across the desert.

Breathlessly she burst onto the balcony, leaned against the wall and wondered if her heart would ever stop its pounding. Perspiration trickled down her cheeks and the palms of her hands were moist. If she stood still, very still, then everything would be right again with her. She was not mad. She must not think she was. It was only— only . . .

The tiles of the roof extended over the balcony, and into her vision came the scarlet color against the dazzling sky. And it was then that she saw them, the three black, furry legs reaching out uncertainly, and she watched with a kind of numb fascination until they retracted into the nested tile edge of the roof. A tarantula? she wondered calmly knowing that there was a time—only yesterday—when the creature would have caused her to gasp and even cry out in fright, but now? Now she felt nothing at the sight of this desert creature. His presence was unimportant when compared to that—that room from which she had just fled, and the half-crazed, unpredictable girl that was somewhere nearby.

It was at that moment the telephone rang, and from below in the patio, she saw Anita emerge from the second door on the far side and hurry into the house. After a moment, Vickie reentered and stood at the top of the stairs, watching as the girl answered the phone.

"Mrs. Bishop? I will call her." Then seeing Vickie begin to descend, she said. "It is for you."

"Thank you," Vickie replied with relief. It would have to be Phil.

"Vickie," he said, "sorry I left before you were up this morning, but Jim and I decided to come here to see the property. As it turned out that what's her name—Anita's mother had to go to L.A., so Norman took her, but you're still not alone, and—"

"But Phil—"

"Now, hon, you're not going to like this, but I'm at the airport. I have to fly back to San Francisco—"

"You what!"

"Baby, it can't be helped. Lecursi has to sign some papers. He can't leave there. He's in a bind. There's nothing else I can do."

"Wait for me, Phil. I want to go home with you."

"Vickie, the plane leaves in ten minutes. Can't you just relax and enjoy yourself a bit?"

"No. No, I can't. You don't understand."

"Vickie!" Here was that tone of exasperation he used too often.

"When will you come back?" she asked bleakly.

"Tomorrow night, I hope; unless Lecursi suddenly decides to get a little sticky about the price. He didn't sound too happy when I talked to him a few minutes ago on the phone. I have to leave now, and—"

"But, Phil!"

"I have to go, or I'll miss the plane. Bye for now."

There was a click, and standing quite still, she looked at Anita who waited in the entrance to the dining room.

"Was the news bad?" the girl asked.

Vickie replaced the phone. "I don't know. Well—it isn't really. My husband has to fly back home and probably can't return here until tomorrow night."

"Oh. Is there anything I can do?"

Vickie looked thoughtfully at this girl who now seemed as composed as if the episode in the kitchen had never taken place. "Anita, do you know if our car is still here, or is that the one they drove?"

"I don't know, but we can see," she said.

Near the foot of the stairs, the girl opened the door leading to the patio, and Vickie followed as they walked beneath the balcony. They passed two doors and stopped at the third which Anita opened. Before them was the empty garage. "Did you want to go somewhere?" she asked.

"Yes, but apparently I shall be staying here." Why, she wondered, had Phil and Jim driven separate cars? Strange. "I wanted to fly back to San Francisco," she said.

"You wanted to go home?"

"Yes. Yes, I did."

"How long have you lived there?"

"In San Francisco? Twenty-seven years. All of my life."

"Oh! You cannot be that old."

"Mmmm." This was the kind of left-handed compliment to which Vickie could never quite find the right answer.

"I—I am though," she said. "Well . . . " She placed her hands out before her in a gesture of helplessness. "I should have brought a book with me."

"We have a few here. Mr. Burant does not read often. Would you like to go for a walk?"

"A walk?"

"Yes, in the desert. But then you might not like that. The sun is warm and bright today. Too bright maybe. It might scorch your skin."

"Quite likely. I do sunburn easily."

"I have a sombrero you could wear. Wait here. I'll get it."

With misgivings Vickie watched the girl cross the patio and enter her room on the other side. What a bewildering person she was, Vickie thought. There was an appealing, almost pathetic quality about her, but then there was this— illness. Vickie walked over to the well, looked at the elaborate festoon of leaves and flowers wrought from iron, reached up and touched the bucket, then leaned over to peer into its dark depths.

"Mrs. Bishop!"

Vickie, startled, stepped back and stared at Anita who stood wearing a look of terror. "You must not go near the well—ever."

"Whatever do you mean?"

"The well. Stand back. That is where—where—"

"Where what?" Vickie asked, trying to keep her voice from trembling.

Anita was approaching her slowly, sombrero in hand. "There is water in the well," she said. "It is very deep and there is water at the bottom. It is dark down there and . . . "

"And what?"

"Shall we go now, Mrs. Bishop?"

Vickie took a deep breath and reached out for the hat

being offered her. Shall we go now? Shall I go walking across this wild, alien place with a girl who is a victim of an unbalanced mind? She followed her, however, and watched as Anita opened an unlocked gate in the wall at the back. Better to humor her, Vickie was thinking, better to do as she wants.

Outside the wall she hesitated momentarily and looked at the scene of vastness before them. What if the girl should become violent? What then? Her eyes spanned the endless miles of uninhabited land. There would be no one—no one at all. And now they were walking, saying nothing.

At last Vickie had to break the disturbing silence that seemed a monstrous thing. "I hope there are no rattlers out here."

"We will be careful," the girl said.

"I saw a huge spider in the roof tiles a while ago, or rather three of its legs. I wonder if it could be a tarantula?"

"Their bite is not harmful."

"It doesn't need to be," Vickie said. "The sight of the creature is enough to frighten a person to death."

"There are more frightening things."

Vickie pretended she did not know what Anita meant. "Yes, I dare say there are. Snakes . . . Scorpions."

The silence returned and they walked on. Vickie was alert, watching each shadow, each fleeting movement of insect life, but mostly she watched the girl at her side.

This time it was Anita who ended the silence. "There is a wolf-spider on the desert that has eight eyes; six on its face and two on the top of its head."

"Oh! If one is nearby," Vickie said, "I'd rather not see it."

"You will not, but it will see you."

"Now there's a comforting thought."

"We are seen many times when we do not know," Anita said in a hushed tone. "Do you ever feel the eyes that watch you—watch everything you do?"

"No. No, of course not." She must veer the conversation to a less dangerous course. "Anita, tell me about yourself. Where are you from?"

"Mr. Burant brought us here, my mother and me, from Los Angeles to work for him and his wife. When I was younger I lived in Mexico with my parents, but after my father died . . . "

"Yes?" Vickie waited, but the girl did not continue and seemed to be lost in thought. On and on they went, and after a time Vickie probed for more information. "How long have you lived here?" she asked, then recalled that Norman had told them this.

"One year, almost."

"Do you intend to stay?"

The girl cast her a quick glance, then shrugged. "My mother, she must work somewhere, and she likes it here."

"But you, Anita. Is this the right life for you?"

There followed another long pause. Finally she spoke. "My mother needs my help—then, too, she should not be left alone in a house where—I mean the way it is. And I cannot leave. I—I am tied here."

It must have been inevitable that they return to this subject that haunted the girl. "Anita, what do you mean about being tied here?" She heard the girl catch her breath, and Vickie waited for an answer that did not come. "The house?" she asked, for here Anita had struck a respondent chord. "What is wrong with the house?" It had been difficult to form the words, for suddenly Vickie's mouth felt dry, very dry. She could not recall ever having felt so thirsty.

"Kathleen," Anita said. "She is still there. I keep begging her and begging her, but she will not rest. Never will she leave me alone. When I see her I run and I pray. And when she calls to me, I hold my hands over my ears."

Vickie's nerves tingled while tiny flecks swam in a turbulence before her eyes. The sky was too bright, the air too crystal clear. Every strange twisted tree and sharp-spined cactus; every round tumbleweed stood motionless, all blending into a picture of brilliance, unreal and alarming. It was as if the world had suddenly come to a stop, nothing lived, nothing moved but the diminutive specks swirling before her. Who is mad, she thought, this girl or I? She must say something, something sane.

"Perhaps it's only a dream you have, Anita. Sometimes we can have the same nightmares repeatedly. You knew Mrs. Burant about six months?"

"Yes. And it is not a dream. She still lives. Even though she died."

"Oh, Anita! Honestly." A shiver surged through her. How frightening this girl was!

"It is true," Anita said quietly.

"You say you have seen her. Has your mother seen her, also?"

"I think she has, but she says no. She is afraid though and whispers, 'Madre de Dios, please help her.' "

The woman must pray for her own sick daughter, Vickie thought, not for the phantom that lingers here. She drew in her breath. Am I beginning to believe this girl's story she wondered?

"She thinks I am possessed by the evil one to see what I see."

"You know better than that. It must be a shadow, a kind of mirage that you see." Hallucinating, Vickie thought and while pity tempered the fear she felt, the world began to live again. Wind, like a soft warm breath crossed the sand and with it the motionless stillness was broken. A tumbleweed rolled a little, and the breeze whispered into

Vickie's ear and toyed with a wisp of her hair like the fingers and voice of a gentle lover.

"No!" the girl cried out. "I see her! I do! You are just like Jim. He is blinded, too, and will not believe me. He becomes so angry with me."

Quickly Vickie stepped aside and almost into some thorny brushwood that seemed to reach out for her. The fear was back stronger than before. She wanted to scream and run.

"Look over there," Anita cried, and pointed toward distant lavender hills. "That is where she died. That is where she wandered away and was lost."

Vickie saw the way the girl stared at the low rise in the distance. She dared not take her own eyes from this bedeviled, tortured creature.

"Jim tried to find her, and he did," the girl was saying, "but he was too late."

Now the girl turned, gripped Vickie's arm, and her eyes seemed to be burning with a fiery glow as she stared at her. "I saw him bring her back," she cried as if in pain. "He had her in his car, and her skin was—and her tongue—" She released her grip and placed both her hands over her eyes as if to block out the image that was there. "Did you—did you ever see anyone who had died of thirst?" she asked with a moan.

Slowly Vickie backed away. "I—I think we should go back to the house," she said, and for one cold moment thought that Anita was going to reach out again and detain her. "I've had enough sun."

After a moment, Anita turned and together they retraced their steps. "A helicopter came and many cars, but it was Jim who found her. She died of thirst. Did you know that?"

Vickie nodded. "Yes, you told me."

"That's why she stands there and looks down."

"Stands where?" Vickie asked, cold with horror.

"At the well, just as you did. And she looks down into the dark water. Just as you were doing. She died of thirst, you know."

Vickie tried to hurry now, but walking in the sand was far different from the pavements to which she had become accustomed. It seemed as if she would never get back to the house, her feet were leaden as though in a bad dream.

"Why do you try to hurry so?" Anita asked.

Yes, why? Vickie wondered. She was becoming as terrified of the house as this poor girl. "The sun, and I'm hungry, I think." She was thirsty too, but could not voice the word.

"Do you hear it?" the girl said, as she once again gripped Vickie's arm. "Listen!"

The soft breeze was quickly becoming a wind. "Yes," Vickie said. "I like the sound of wind. I'm used to it."

"Not the wind," the girl said almost angrily. "Listen! It blows from the hills back there, and carries her voice to us. Hear her calling?"

"Yes," Vickie lied, and saw the anger cool in the girl's eyes and felt her grip lessen.

"She calls to him."

"Her husband?"

"Yes."

"But has he ever heard her?"

"I do not think so, but I hear her often, and it is so sad it tears at my heart."

There should be three in the car leaving here, Vickie was thinking. She and Phil should not leave this girl behind, destined to madness by these diabolical tricks of her imagination. This place, this house, was too far removed from life. Unhealthy. Conducive to mental illness for the susceptible. Then she thought of what it had been doing to her, and she winced inwardly.

When they reached the house, they found they were still alone. Vickie was disappointed that Jim Burant had not returned. How she would have welcomed his affable manner at this moment! With a sigh of resignation, she assisted Anita in the kitchen preparing sandwiches, fruit and tea. As they worked she told her of San Francisco, describing it graphically, talking and talking, giving Anita no chance to speak of the terror that had become a part of her.

"I really think," she told the girl, "that you should leave here; move back to Los Angeles, perhaps."

"I have told you, I cannot do that."

"If you really wanted to, I'm sure something could be worked out. You might like San Francisco."

Anita stared thoughtfully out of the window above the sink.

"You shouldn't stay here."

"But there is my mother, and there is . . . "

"Would your mother object to your leaving?"

"No. No, she might not. But she would miss me, and . . . " She gave a kind of helpless little laugh.

"May I ask how old you are, Anita?"

"Twenty."

"Talk to your mother about it. She'll want you to go where you'll be happy." Vickie raised her teacup as in a toast. "A new life for Anita," she said, and saw a hesitant smile appear on the girl's lips, but she also saw Anita's hand tremble as she raised her cup, and there was no smile in her eyes.

2

IT WAS ONE o'clock when Jim's car entered the garage, and soon he joined them in the kitchen. "I hope I'm in time for lunch," he said.

Anita smiled at him. What a pretty girl she was when she smiled, Vickie noticed; when that look of haunting fear was gone. "Yes, you are. We have sandwiches, but would you like soup, also?" Her voice was soft when she spoke to him, and now Vickie wondered. Was the girl in love with Jim?

"I think I would," he replied. "That is, if it's not too much bother."

"No bother. There is plenty left from yesterday; enough for all."

"Fine." He sat down across from Vickie, smiled and let his eyes linger on her.

"Where is Phil's car, at the airport?" she asked.

He nodded. "Waiting for his return," he told her.

"How fortunate that you took both cars," she said. Here was a thought that had hovered somewhere in her mind all morning. Had Phil known he might have to fly home?

"Wasn't it though?" he remarked. "We knew there might be the necessity of making the flight."

"I see."

"I'm willing to sell—at the right price. But there are some details to be ironed out, as always. Your husband is a good salesman."

"Yes, I suppose he is."

"He sold himself to you."

She laughed quietly and searched for an answer that evaded her. These lines were not in the script, and she had never been adept at ad-libbing. She was thankful for a sudden blast of wind that thrust itself against the house at that moment. There was no need to reply to his comment.

"Damn!" he boomed. "I think we're in for a sandstorm."

"Do they occur often?" she asked.

"Quite often."

"But—you must like living here."

"I really do like the desert," he replied. "A man can move and breathe out here. You can be free to have solitude or raise hell. Our lives are our own. We have privacy, complete privacy. Cities give me claustrophobia. If it gets too dull, I drive down to Palm Springs. All winter there's plenty of action there."

As the three sat at the table, Vickie was conscious of the amiability of this man; it reached out and wrapped itself around her like a warm cape in a cold fog. And it would give her the courage to speak to him of a situation which she knew was really no business of hers. The opportunity came a little later while she and Jim sat together before a fire he had built in the living room. With the dancing flames, the character of this room changed so drastically that her experience this morning seemed inconceivable. Had it really happened? Oh, God! She mustn't doubt her own sanity.

"I—seldom meddle," she began hesitantly, "and dislike those who do, however. . . . " She looked up at him, this tall man who stood before the fireplace with the blaze at his back. "I'm probably out of line discussing this with you, but. . . . " Out of line indeed, she thought. If Phil were here, he'd murder me. "It's Anita." There, she had begun and she must continue. "This morning we had breakfast together and went for a walk."

"Good," he said.

She shook her head. "But it wasn't. Not at all. I found her to be—well, frankly, mentally disturbed. She's sick, and she needs help, badly."

"Oh, that."

"Then you know?"

"Vickie, I hardly think she's sick, but there is a tendency there toward hysteria." He shook his head, and smiled. "The truth is, she has one hell of an imagination, to the point where you can't believe everything she says."

"But she believes it, and that is what must be changed. Have you ever seen that anguish and terror in her eyes?"

He nodded, turned then and faced the frenzied dance of fire writhing in spears from the logs. She could no longer see his face. She had gone too far, had said too much.

"What has Anita told you?" he asked.

"Nothing."

Quickly he looked at her over his shoulder. "Vickie?" He made her feel like a small child keeping secrets from her parents. "Tell me what she has been saying to you."

"I've said too much already," she replied. "After all none of this is any of my business."

"But—how can I help her unless I know what is worrying her? You did tell me she needed help, didn't you?"

"She does."

"Anguish and terror, you said. What frightens her? What makes her suffer?"

"Do you mean you don't know? Hasn't she ever discussed it with you?"

"I'm not sure. She—well, she thinks this house is haunted. As I say, she's imaginative, superstitious and needs to move away from here. Needs to be with others her own age."

"With that, I agree," Vickie declared. "This is no place for her. Have you talked to her mother about it?"

He shook his head. "It wouldn't do any good."

"But why not? I don't understand."

"Because Anita would not want to leave here."

The subject seemed to have come to a temporary halt, and the only sounds were those of the crackling fire and the moaning of the wind as it swept the sand into a tumult outside the house. Jim crossed the room and closed the draperies. "Sand will seep in no matter what," he said, "but it helps a little to keep the windows covered." He walked then to the candelabra, and slowly, as in a ritual, touched a match to each tall, thick candle.

Now there were the shadows, and this time they swayed with the wavering lights from the fireplace and the candles. Vickie watched as though hypnotized. It seemed that she and Jim no longer were the only occupants of this room. There were the crouching, moving forms behind the chairs, the sofa, the tables, the piano. There were moments when arms of darkness would reach out along the floor, or the draperies, or Jim's back, only to vanish at the whim of a flame in the fireplace.

"How long have you and Phil been married, Vickie?" And the question quickly brought her back to reality.

"—Five years."

"Happy ones?"

Her proper line would be, "Of course." And she should raise her eyebrows at the effrontery of his inquiry. But somehow the drama had gone astray. There was this vague sense of confusion. She was forgetting her lines, and it no longer seemed to matter. "Yes and no," she said.

"You're very frank. I like that. Candor isn't too common in a woman."

She laughed. He was teasing her. "Really, sir!" she said mockingly.

"And I like you," he added.

"Thank you."

"But you'll not like what I'm going to say next."

Her eyes widened as she looked at him and the flickering shadows playing upon his face. "And what is that?"

"I don't like your husband."

I should rise and leave the room, she thought, but instead she sat very still, waiting.

"He's a fool."

"What are you trying to do?" she asked. "Anger me? If so, why?"

"No," he said, moving toward the bar. "I'm only trying to tell you something, but—apparently I can't. At least, not yet. Do you have any scruples about drinking before five in the afternoon?"

"No," she replied, "not under the present circumstances."

"Good. We have an excuse, haven't we? Present circumstances. What better reason to have a drink could there ever be, than present circumstances? A martini for you. A martini for me. Oh, what an afternoon this could be! Like my little rhyme?"

"Not particularly."

He laughed. "Vickie, there is something Victorian about

you. You're a dual personality. You are the warm, lovable Vickie at times, but definitely the prim and proper Victoria at others. You're damn interesting. Phil is a lucky devil, but doesn't know it."

She said nothing and after a moment he offered her the drink. She avoided his eyes as she took it. Somehow the present circumstances seemed to have changed so suddenly that they became a reason for not imbibing. She expected him to sit beside her on the sofa, but instead he stretched out luxuriously on a chair across from her and looked thoughtfully at the liquid in his glass that reflected the flames in myriad colors.

"Did you know I lost my wife? She died six months ago."

"Yes, I was told. I'm sorry."

"Thank you. And you have brought it all back to me, her death, you know. And to her brother Norman, also. I can tell by the way he looks at you."

"I don't understand."

"The similarity. She was small like you. Her eyes were green like yours. But her hair was more blonde—I mean less red."

She frowned. It was as if she had lived this moment before. Then she remembered. It had been Anita who had spoken these same words.

"You are alike," he said. "I mean, she was like you in other ways as well. The same personality more or less."

"That's interesting," she said. He had almost talked of her as though she still lived, just as Anita had done. Vickie took more than a sip of the martini. She must warm the strange chill that was closing around her.

"Is the drink okay?" he asked.

"Perfect, thank you."

"Kathleen was impulsive," he went on, "and sometimes did foolish things."

"We all do," she said.

"But this trait cost her her life."

He lifted the glass to his lips and took several swallows. "She ran off. She ran out of the house and across the desert—alone—without water, without anything. It was August and hot. She must have lost her mind."

"Didn't anyone see her leave?"

"I had gone to Los Angeles on business, Anita was taking care of her mother who was ill. After a time she realized that Kathleen was not around, and while she had not seen her leave, she assumed she had just missed seeing her drive away."

"How dreadful!"

"She didn't become concerned, because Kathleen frequently drove to Palm Springs or somewhere without telling Anita or her mother that she was leaving. It was not until the following morning, that Anita began to look through the house and the garage, where she found Kathleen's car still there."

"What did she do?"

"Called the highway patrol, and the search began. I knew nothing of her disappearance until I returned that night. They even used a helicopter, roads were checked, the airlines, the bus terminals." He lifted the glass to his lips and drained it. "We looked everywhere," he said, "except where she was."

He walked back to the bar, refilled his glass and sat down again. "I don't know when we would have found her if it had not been for the—the buzzards."

She winced.

"Forgive me, Vickie. I shouldn't have told you all this." She said nothing as he emptied his glass. "Do you need a refill?" he asked.

"No, thank you." Is he going to tell me why she ran

away? she wondered. For some reason she hoped he would not.

"There are women like that," he said, "and then there are the others. The wise and calculating. They scare me."

So you're not afraid of me, she was thinking. I'm neither wise, nor calculating. Like Kathleen, I am foolish. She took a large swallow of her drink. It burned a little.

"What are you thinking, Vickie?"

"Oh, nothing," she replied.

"That's not true. I can see the wheels turning like crazy."

"I was thinking about Kathleen's death."

"I don't want to talk of it anymore," he said firmly. He mixed another drink and turned to her. "Now let's talk about you."

"Very well. Let's begin with your telling me whatever it was that you were hesitant about revealing, at least at this time. I want to know what it was."

"Oh, that."

"Yes, and why you don't like Phil and think him a fool."

"And that, too?"

"Yes."

"Ah, curiosity," he said, "a typical feminine trait, and a disastrous one, too often." He mixed more martinis, and this time, with the shaker in hand, he sat down at her side, filled her glass to the brim, then placed the shaker on the table before them.

"Naturally you want to know why I said what I did. To tell you the truth, I'm not sure why I said it. I haven't one fact to back up the thought that was in my mind and making me angry. It must have been one of those intuitive things. As a woman you should understand that kind of thinking."

He was close to her, too close. She began to move away,

but suddenly his hands were on her shoulders and he was kissing her; a soft, lingering kiss that immobilized her with a warm, pleasant flush. "Phil doesn't love you," he was whispering, "but I do. It hit me like an explosion the first time we met.

"Vickie, Vickie," he murmured, and she jumped to her feet. She saw the flash of a red skirt in the doorway, then it was gone. Anita! Anita had seen them! "Oh, Jim," she gasped. "You shouldn't have done that."

Quickly she placed her glass on the table and hurried from the room. Now she was running on tiptoe along the hall. When she reached the door to the patio, she saw the girl fleeing toward her room, the wind carrying her long hair out behind her like a banner of black.

Vickie walked out into the patio, closed the door behind her and stood beneath the balcony. She had been right. Anita was in love with Jim. That was the reason she wouldn't leave this house. Turning her face against the wind, Vickie crossed the flagstones and stopped outside the girl's door. "Anita," she called. "Please let me in. I want to talk to you."

There was no answer.

"Anita, please. What you saw was nothing, really. It didn't mean a thing, except that Jim has had a little too much to drink."

Still there was no response, and Vickie shuddered with the thought of what this girl, with her tormented mind, must be suffering. She tapped on her door. Then she rapped firmly. The torments of jealousy. How would she react? Vickie wondered. "Anita, please!"

With a sigh, Vickie hurried toward the well. She would sit in its shelter from the wind, wait on the stones that surrounded it. Surely Anita would open her door after a moment, curious to see if she still waited outside.

The door, however, did not open, and neither did the one leading into the hallway. Jim had not followed her. As sand slowly drifted into the patio, it seemed to Vickie that she and the sand and the wind were the only forms of life left on this parched earth. At least they moved. Apparently Jim still sat on the sofa. What were his thoughts? And Anita still remained in her room. Did she lie across her bed shedding futile tears? Was she sulking in a chair? Then a new thought came to Vickie. Was the girl inside the door seething with rage? With this thought, Vickie rose to her feet. She could still feel the grip of the girl's hand on her arm.

Shading her eyes against the wind, Vickie turned and looked down into the darkness of the well. The water, so far below, mirrored her image. Fascinated, she stared at it, then saw that the reflection did not produce an accurate picture. The face was not quite right, and the hair was more blonde—less red. It was not her face.

With horror she straightened up, then with a cry reached for the iron bower over the well and held with all her might. She was being pushed forward, shoved with a force like a blast of the wind! What pressed against her, however, was not the wind, for it had not altered its course. And then as suddenly as this powerful thrust had been born it died, and Vickie stood trembling, the sand blowing into her face, the sharp petals and leaves from the wrought iron cutting into the palms of her hands.

She knew before she turned her head to look, that Anita was not there. Vickie stood alone in the patio. Alone? she wondered. But, am I?

Enveloped with an icy terror, she fled. When she reached the hallway, she did not stop, but continued to run up the stairs, out onto the balcony and to her room. As she opened her door, she paused for a moment and looked below. Anita's door was still closed. Sand still rippled along the flagstones, and the bucket swayed back and forth over the well as the wind blew from the direction of the distant hills. Did she hear a name being called? Oh, God! she thought. No. Such things don't exist. She entered her room, bolted the door and threw herself onto the bed. Her heart was pounding so, it seemed ready to tear out of her body. It was some time before she sank into a fitful sleep.

3

IT WAS FIVE in the afternoon before Vickie rose from the bed, showered and changed her clothes. As she left the room she noticed how dark the waning day had become, and how the wind's intensity had increased. Below her the palms in their redwood containers waved and danced in a frenzied kind of way, and she knew that a sound she heard would be that of the bucket over the well as it was blown against the wrought iron. She did not look at it, only hurried along the balcony not stopping until she reached the upstairs hall. Here she paused for a moment, took a deep breath and with a mask of serenity on her face, descended the stairs. The part she must play this evening was one of concealment, of hiding emotions stirring within her, of pretending that nothing, nothing at all unusual had taken place.

Below she found Norman just entering the house, closing the front door firmly behind him. His eyes went directly to the stairway and he smiled. "Hello, Vickie," he said. "How are you?"

"Fine, thank you. And you?"

"Glad to be back. Driving in this wind isn't easy, and the traffic in and near L.A. was murderous. It's good to keep in practice though. I'll soon be going back."

"Oh, you're from there?"

"That's right. I came here to Jim's retreat for rest and relaxation. Doctor's orders."

"Really?" she replied, thinking that he did not appear to be in need of either. She nodded toward the telephone on a nearby desk. "I wonder if it would be all right for me to use this. I want to call to see if Phil reached home okay."

"Your husband? Did he—leave? I mean did he go—"

She nodded. "It was necessary for him to fly back to San Francisco. Papers to sign, and all that."

"Oh. Oh, I see. Well, certainly. Help yourself." He walked toward the stairs. "See you in a few minutes," he called back, and she saw a kind of quizzical smile on his face as he glanced toward her.

Quickly she dialed the area code and number, hoping to talk to Phil before Jim appeared from somewhere. Anxiously she listened to the ringing. She pictured their phone on the desk near the windows overlooking the bay. The thought made her homesick. How idiotic, she told herself, to feel this way so soon. Answer. Please answer, Phil. Then with a sigh she hung up. He was probably seeing Lecursi. Yes, that would be the logical conclusion, of course. She would try to call him again, later.

Standing in the hallway she was uncertain about where

she should go. Might Jim still be in the living room? Perhaps it would be better to go to the kitchen and offer to help Anita. She was more than reluctant to approach the girl alone, however. Oh, Phil! Why had he gone away leaving her in this situation? But then, how could he have known how things were at this—this desert flower?

"Vickie?"

She turned to see Jim standing in the doorway of the living room. He looked as if he had been sleeping. "Will you accept an apology for my behavior?" he asked. "Shall we say that I—just got carried away?"

His expression was so hesitant that secretly she was a little amused, but then she thought of the pain the incident had brought to Anita, and her voice was sober when she said, "It's quite all right."

"And the things I told you; forget them. Okay?"

"Of course."

He yawned and walked toward the stairway, then stopped and looked back at her. "They were all true, however," he added. "Every damn word." He climbed the steps, and at the top paused for a moment to regard her thoughtfully. She returned his gaze and saw him shrug a little before he vanished.

Puzzling she thought, and forced herself to enter the kitchen where Anita stood at the stove. Quickly she glanced at Vickie, then lowered her eyes. "Are you all right, Anita. I'm so sorry that—"

"I am fine." The girl's voice was low and cold.

"About this afternoon," Vickie said. "I want you to realize that what you saw was not what it seemed to be."

Anita shook her head. "Please. I heard what you said at my door."

"Good. Then you understand. I have just one more thing to say, then we'll not speak of this again. I really feel that you should leave this house as soon as possible. If you want, you may go away with Phil and me tomorrow night." She saw doubt in the girl's eyes. "Anita, if you are in love with Jim, I can assure you you'll get over it more quickly than you realize at this time. Now, what may I do to help prepare dinner?"

"Are you really going to leave tomorrow night?" There was hope in the girl's voice and in her face.

"If not, then the following morning for sure; if I have anything to say about it. Will you come with us?"

"No. I am only glad that you are going. Kathleen has become more restless since you arrived. She was standing at the well again this afternoon beckoning to me. There is something she wants to tell me."

"Oh, Anita!"

"Please leave. I can prepare dinner alone."

Back in the hall, Vickie glanced at her wristwatch. It was a few minutes after six. Should she try to reach Phil again? But no. He would be having cocktails, she supposed, with Lecursi, and perhaps dinner after that. She must be patient.

As she entered the living room she found that the candles had burned down, and the flames that had roared in the fireplace were now smouldering embers. Again she sank onto the sofa and stared with unseeing eyes at the cocktail shaker and glasses that had not been removed from the table. In her mind was pictured the figure of a woman standing at the well, a woman whose small white hand motioned toward a terrified girl. Vickie shivered and sat quite still as though afraid to move, to attract attention, to make her presence known to—to whatever might be nearby. How contagious this fear was that gripped Anita and now her.

It seemed to Vickie as if the two men would never join her, never release her from this immobility that was like death itself. Then at last they did, entering the room almost simultaneously.

"The cocktail hour," Jim announced in his usual jovial manner. "Excuse me while I get ice from the kitchen."

Norman dropped heavily into a chair. "I've really had a day," he said, leaning back and looking at Vickie thoughtfully.

She studied his face, his eyes. What are his thoughts, she wondered? Why do I feel as though his purpose here is sinister? Why do I feel that he is waiting for something to take place, something of which I cannot conceive? What does he expect to happen? She saw him rise, reach for the poker and prod a log of the wavering fire, causing sparks of red and orange and blue to explode with loud crackling sounds. He sat down again, saying nothing, only looking at her. It was becoming embarrassing. "Uh—what kind of work do you do?" she asked, to break the stillness.

"I have a chain of restaurants." Then after a moment, "How do you spend your days, Vickie?"

"I have a shop. Interiors."

"A decorator. Interesting?"

She nodded. "Usually. I like it."

"How did you get into that line of work?"

"I inherited the business from an aunt. I used to work with her during summer vacations and . . . " She shrugged. "I just—kind of fell into it."

"But not without artistic talent," he told her.

Then Jim was back. He placed a bowl of ice cubes on the bar and looked from one of his guests to the other. "Well, name your poison."

"Thank you, but I don't believe I want anything," Vickie replied.

"Oh, but you have to have something. I insist," Jim told her. "I will gladly mix up anything you want."

She smiled at him, but shook her head.

"I could use a scotch and soda," Norman said. "Do you like scotch, Vickie?"

"Yes, but I—"

"Then scotch it is," Jim stated. "I can't enjoy drinking in the company of those who don't. Two scotch and sodas coming up and a vodka for me."

After serving them, he sat down in the other chair across from her, and looking at his face, Vickie decided that he drank too much. Was it to help him forget Kathleen? "I forgot to ask you earlier," she said, "but are things going in a way to please you?"

Jim's expression seemed uncertain as he glanced at her, and she read a wariness in his eyes. "What do you mean?" he asked.

"The sale in Palm Springs; the motel. It is a motel, isn't it?"

"Oh—yes. Yes, all we really need now is your husband's client's name on the dotted. What is that name again? It's an odd one, as I recall. Began with a C or an S, I think."

"Lecursi, Barton K.," she said. "A new client, incidentally."

"Oh, yes. That's the name. That's it."

Vickie gazed into her glass. Strange, she thought. Phil had said Lecursi had been here, hadn't he? The man had even described this house to Phil, but had not done it justice.

"Let's drink to the successful closing of the deal," Jim said, and two glasses were raised. Norman, Vickie saw, did not join in the toast. What lies hidden behind that enigmatic facade, she wondered. And his silence, how uncomfortable it made her. Except for the spurting of the fire on the hearth, the stillness seemed to be everywhere, and again she broke it.

"I offered to help Anita prepare dinner," she said. "With her mother away, I—I thought. . . . But she preferred that I didn't."

"She needs no help," Jim told her. "Anita's really very capable. Besides, I like having you right here. You bring something to the room that is needed, doesn't she, Norm?"

Norman nodded. "Like a lovely Dresden China figurine," he replied, his eyes on hers meditatively.

Vickie thanked him, but wondered if he meant to be sarcastic. How out of place such an ornament would be in this room! Had his remark carried a message? She considered this possibility a moment. Could it be that he was telling her she should not be here?

"This is such a handsome house," she said. "And incidentally, I'm interested in the well. I mean, it seems such an unlikely place to find one."

"The well isn't for real," Jim told her. "It was a whim of Kathleen's. She wanted one, so I had it dug and water piped in. Actually it's purely decorative."

"It's certainly a very attractive addition," she said. "I suppose it isn't deep, the water, I mean."

He shook his head. "Not unless you fell into it," he said laughingly. "There is probably eight or nine feet of it. The well itself was dug to twice that depth, as I recall. The potted palms were Kathleen's wish also, but they don't thrive on this high desert. It's too cold here in the winter. She liked to refer to the patio as her oasis, especially during the hot months of summer. And they are hot."

Vickie pictured the young woman who had been his wife. The day when she vanished would have been one with the heat rising in shimmering waves from the desert sand, and the fiery August sun would have hammered on her head as she wandered in one direction and then another. Under such circumstances anyone could easily become confused about directions. Vickie frowned. No water. No shade. Lost and alone. She shuddered.

Anita appeared in the doorway to announce dinner, and there was a note of kindness in Jim's voice as he thanked her. Vickie turned her thoughts from his wife and her horrible death and with the men entered the dining room. She found herself seated in the same chair as the night before, and was more aware of the windows behind her than the meal that the girl was serving in a slow, rather mechanical way. How at ease she is, Vickie thought. How very relaxed. Anita did not even seem to hear the way the wind was feeling the window panes like hands persistently patting and tapping, seeking a way to enter. But soon, Vickie saw that she was mistaken. The disinterested robot-like motions the girl displayed, were apparently caused by the cold rigidity of an almost paralyzing fear that her eyes could not conceal.

Anita did hear the tapping, Vickie realized, and quickly she glanced at Jim and then Norman. Were they deaf? Were they pretending not to be aware of anything outside the house? Someone was there, someone who wanted in. What was wrong? Why didn't they look up from their plates, puzzled, as they should be? Oh, God! she thought. Is it only Anita and I who hear?

Jim was looking at her. "What's the matter?" he asked. "Are you chilly?"

"No—" Vickie breathed. "I—I'm fine."

"You look cold," he said, rising and coming around the table to her. "The wind does creep in a bit around the windows." Now he was picking up her plate, silver and glasses. "Sit over here between us. We'll keep you warm."

Gladly she moved to the other side where Norman now stood behind a chair that was to be hers. "How lucky I am," she said, forcing herself to laugh lightly, hoping this would hide the tremor in her voice. "Two handsome men to assist me, to see that I'm warm and comfortable."

Her eyes met Norman's as he pulled the chair back for her, and she was surprised to find a look of deep concern there. Did he know why she had found sitting with her back to the windows disturbing? Had he sensed what she was feeling? If so, surely he would conclude that she was as sick as Anita, if he knew of the girl's aberrations.

"I did seem to become a bit chilled over there," she said.

"This is better. Thank you."

Her eyes rose to Anita's and a message seemed to pass between them. The girl knew what Vickie had heard. She knew and understood.

Following dinner they returned to the living room where Norman went directly to the piano. "Does anyone object?" he asked. "I'm not good, but I can help stave off the howling of the wind."

"Please do," Vickie said and took a chair near the piano. She relaxed a little as his fingers traveled expertly over the keyboard filling the room with numbers from several current musicals. "Oh, you play beautifully," she told him, as she listened entranced. No longer was he the quiet one, the audience. He was onstage now, centered in the spotlight. Had it been her imagination, or was there a difference in this man since he returned from Los Angeles? Somehow, suddenly he had come alive.

Then Jim was before her, reaching for her hand and pulling her to her feet. "Dance with me, Vickie," he said, and she saw the face at the piano darken momentarily with the shadow of a frown. The brother of the dead Kathleen did not enjoy seeing his brother-in-law with another woman in his arms. This became more evident when the music quickly changed from popular to classical. She felt Jim's body tighten almost imperceptively with irritation. "Apparently the dance is over," he muttered in her ear.

Anita appeared at the door. "You are wanted on the phone," she said.

"Me?" Vickie asked hopefully. Her eyes bright.

"It is for Mr. Burant."

"Excuse me, Vickie," he said, and once again she sat near the piano. Norman's eyes, she found, were looking at her questioningly.

"What would you like to hear?" he asked softly.

"*Clair de Lune,*" she replied.

He nodded. "You're the romantic type. I've suspected it all along. Incurably romantic—and vulnerable."

She did not reply, she only listened while a dreaminess swept over her as the music carried her far away. She was not even aware of Jim's reentrance into the room, but after a moment she saw him there and the mood was gone, the spell broken.

"How about a drink?" he asked. "Crème de menthe or kahlua?"

Now the piano was silent, and she no longer was far away. She was here where the wind shrieked like a crazed monster and she could visualize it shattering the windows, blasting into the room and burying them under tons of sand, thick and smothering against the wall. She listened as it threatened and goaded, called and then—God help her, she thought, somewhere there was the sound of laughter.

"Don't listen," Norman was saying, and startled she stared at him. Then quickly he turned the conversation to their lives and their work. She had to talk about her shop, and the many idiosyncrasies of various members of her clientele. Norman spoke briefly about his restaurants, and Jim, in his own words spoke of "dabbling in real estate."

As they talked, Vickie became more and more aware of the animosity existing between these men. They were courteous, they maintained a pretense of an amicable relationship, but she could detect the hostility running like an undercurrent, strong and grim. She wondered if the reason might be Anita—or Kathleen. Her eyes went from one man to the other and then came the suspicion that something insidious was taking place, something in which she was involved. But no, she told herself. She must control such thoughts.

How could she be involved, she reasoned? What was she reading into their actions, their words? Norman's eyes were speculative, his manner mysterious. And Jim. His face was one of warmth and a certain placidness. His was not the portrait of a guilty man, but then it did not show sorrow either. Did each man wear a mask? If there was some reason for Norman to become suspicious about the death of his sister. . . . Yes, this would account for the aura of distrust that hung between them.

Nervously Vickie fingered a lock of her hair, curling it then releasing it again. Suddenly she stood up. "I—I think I shall go to bed," she said, "and thank you both for a lovely evening." She looked at Jim. "I would like to try again to call Phil. May I?"

"Of course, Vickie, and good night."

As she sat at the small desk and dialed the number she wondered if Phil was watching T.V. As the ringing went on and on she glanced at her wrist watch. Perhaps he was still with Lecursi. She wished he had called her. It would have made her feel so much better.

At last she hung up with disappointment and uncertainty. It was not late, not really, but it wasn't early either. He should be at their apartment, tired and ready to end a long, and what must have been a strenuous day.

She stood up and looked at the shadows grown dark and hanging like yards of tulle in the corners and under the stairs. It was disturbing to have been left here with these people. How little she knew about them, these strange occupants of this house, and yet—how much! With a shiver she hurried toward the stairway and quickly ascended. She would sleep and bring an end to this day. And tomorrow? Phil would call. He had to.

4

WHEN VICKIE REACHED the balcony she slowed her pace while her eyes focused involuntarily upon the well. She froze, stared, blinked and looked again. It couldn't be. Anita's beliefs had taken their effect, she realized, as she hurried toward her room. There had been a fleeting instant when she, too, had seemed to see a figure standing down there, but surely it had been only a shadow, blue and soft, cast by the arch and bucket in the moonlight.

Inside her room she undressed, turned off her light then pulled open the draperies unveiling the dark vista beyond the window. The storm had diminished somewhat. She lay on the bed and looked at the gloom until at last, she slept.

Again however, as she had done during the night before, she wakened—troubled. Eerie moans came from around her and with a gasp, she sat upright and listened. After a moment, and with a flood of relief, came the realization that it was only the wind that had resumed its wailing with a low, hollow and mournful tone. She went to the window and watched the sand moving in such a way that she thought of rippling water on a silver lake. She gazed, fascinated, with the same awe that she had always felt at the witchery of the ocean at home. At home. She sighed, and then, thinking of the shadow at the well, her curiosity moved her across the room where she opened the door a few inches to look down into the patio. She hated herself for checking, not wanting to admit that there could possibly be an apparition, but then . . .

Almost instantly her attention was drawn to the door of Anita's room, for it had opened and closed again, and the form of a man stepped from the darkness beneath the balcony. For a moment Vickie did not breathe as she stood motionless, watching and waiting. He crossed the flagstone silently, entered the house, and a moment later emerged onto the balcony. Like a dark shadow he moved toward the third room across from where she stood and entered it, closing the door softly behind him. There was no mistaking the man's identity. It was Jim Burant.

Vickie took a deep breath as she returned to her bed, sat down, and exhaled slowly. Filtering through her mind were some of the words Anita had spoken.

"She blames me for what happened to her."

"Kathleen hates me."

"She will kill me."

Vickie wondered if this intimacy had begun before Kathleen's death. She sat deep in thought, looking into the night with the contemplative expression while outside the storm again became a frenzied thing, increasing with an alarming force. A thousand hands slapped against her window, and fingers of sand scratched and clawed the glass to gain entrance.

She crawled quickly under the covers and pulled a blanket close around her. She shivered with apprehension as she wondered how much Norman might know and what he might do. What was the plan taking shape in his mind? What were the emotions seething there?

Suddenly in the midst of the wild wind's clamor rose another sound—a rapping at her door. Terrified she jumped up wondering if Jim had seen her watching him. Oh, no! she thought. Again the insistent rapping came, softly she edged nearer the door.

"Who—is it?"

There was no reply, only the knocking that she thought would never stop.

She swallowed with difficulty, then raised her voice and called again. "Who's there? Please answer me."

Could the person not hear because of the wind? She moved to the door, then saw with mounting fear that she had not slipped the bolt into place. At the same moment she noticed something else that caused her to step back and stare. The knob was turning! Then with a blast of wind and stinging sand the door burst open.

Vickie's left hand flew to her face to protect her eyes, and she dared not breathe nor open her mouth to release the scream that seemed to have caught in her throat. With her other hand, she groped out to reach the door, to close it against what was standing there. And when she did, she braced her back against it and fought the wave of darkness and cold that pressed close around her, trying to control the shaking that had taken over her body. Oh, no, she thought. No! It can't be. But for that startling moment while the door was open, she had seen, and would see forever the figure in clouds of blue mist, and the pale golden hair that was blowing across a face in the darkness.

It seemed forever that she stood there unable to move, too cold, too rigid, too—dead. She was fighting now. She must live. She must breathe. She must gain control of herself. Then after a time she groped her way across the room trying to turn on one lamp and then another only to be met with darkness. Someone help me, she thought. This *has* to be a nightmare. She gripped her hands together and tried desperately to regain her senses.

There was no power, no electrical power. That was it. The storm had blown down the lines, of course. There had to be a logical answer to everything, she told herself. Even for what was outside her door. She returned to her bed, keeping her eyes open, for if she closed them she knew she would see again that form, the phantom that was—what? Kathleen? I shall not believe that there are such things, she vowed. I refuse to become chained by fear, as Anita is. I will not allow myself to dwell on the possibility of such a being.

She stared out the window as she contemplated the alternative. Someone was trying to frighten her. This was the only possible answer. But who and why?

Sleep came fitfully after that, and when she dozed it was to dream. Once she was on a train speeding with a deafening clatter through the night, and from its window she saw a station where dim lights revealed the lone figure of a man standing there, a man she recognized. "Phil! Phil!" she called out excitedly, but he turned toward her with unknowing eyes. A stranger? She was a stranger to him, one who was being whisked away from his side with unbelievable speed. "It is me, Vickie!" she cried out and woke, shaking and tearful. Then later in a second flight of terror, her mind carried her to the lavender hills where a young woman made her way laboriously over sand that whirled around her, choking and blinding. As Vickie watched, the woman clawed into it, digging madly, and she knew that it was Kathleen searching for water. She ran toward the struggling form and when she reached her, the woman looked up. It was not Kathleen! It was her own face that stared back at her, and with a cry of horror, Vickie wakened to find a strange pale orange hue outside the window and a choking veil of sand within the room.

The storm was a thing of terror, and she jumped from her bed to dress quickly and hurry to the main part of the house. Once outside the door she ran but a short distance along the balcony where she nearly collided with Norman who was stepping from the room next to hers. "What a morning!" he said, then ran with her to the upstairs hall.

"Whew!" he exclaimed, as he closed the door behind them. "This wind, we could do without. Did you sleep well last night?"

She gave him a quick glance. "No. No, I'm afraid I didn't. How about you?" She watched his face closely.

He was shaking his head. "I can't blame the storm, however," he said. "I haven't slept well for months. Insomnia is a curse, wouldn't you say?"

"I don't know. Perhaps it is."

They were descending the stairs when halfway down he paused and placed a hand on her arm. "Vickie," he said in a hushed voice, "call your husband now, before he leaves your home."

She raised her eyebrows with surprise.

"I mean, call to tell him about the storm. Don't you think you should?"

Call to see if he is there, Norman was thinking, she told herself. And what business is it of his?

"I—I intended to try to reach him," she replied coolly, "but I doubt if the storm would be of interest to him. He doesn't plan to fly back here until tonight, and surely by then . . . "

"Of course, Vickie."

When they reached the hall, she walked directly to the phone while he vanished through the dining room doorway. She dialed their number and as the ringing was repeated again and again without a response, she turned cold with fear and bewilderment. She slowly placed the phone back into its cradle and joined the others in the kitchen.

Anita and Jim were preparing breakfast. On the griddle were eggs, bacon and sliced potatoes. Coffee was perking, and on the table stood four glasses of orange juice, and three lighted candles. The shades were drawn, and it seemed to Vickie as if she had stepped from morning into evening just by crossing the threshold.

"Good morning," the two at the stove said and she returned the greeting. She avoided Norman's eyes, but knew they were watching her questioningly. Since she had joined them this quickly, it was obvious that Phil had not been at home.

As the four of them sat around the table a certain closeness seemed to develop in spite of the complications in their lives, for they had a common enemy, the constant howling wind and their isolation.

"As you have probably noticed, Vickie," said Jim, "we are without electricity."

She nodded. "How long do these sandstorms usually last?"

"As a rule, not too long. This one should blow itself out soon. It doesn't take long for them to do their damage, though. They can take the paint right off a car and pit the glass with a couple of sharp blasts." He looked around him. "They don't do the house any good, either."

"I suppose not," she said, but her thoughts were on Phil's absence from their apartment. Perhaps he was having an early breakfast with Lecursi. He might even be planning on taking an early flight out of San Francisco.

After breakfast she went again to the telephone, and as

before there was no answer to her call. On an impulse she dialed the operator and asked for the number of Barton K. Lecursi in San Francisco. A moment later she was informed that there was no listing for anyone by that name. "But there has to be," she insisted. "My husband knows him well. He's a client of his."

"There is a listing for a Daniel Licursi," the operator told her. "LI, but not LE. Would you want me to ring that number?"

Vickie hesitated. She was so sure of the name, and . . . suddenly a shrill whistle shrieked into her ear and then nothing. "Hello? Hello?" she called.

The line was dead.

Back in the kitchen she sat down again at the table to join the others for a second cup of coffee. She felt their eyes on her questioningly.

"Is there something wrong?" Jim asked. "You have a strange, little girl lost, expression on that pretty face of yours."

She kept her eyes on the coffee before her. How could she tell this man that there was no Barton Lecursi? But there had to be. This was mad. There was some mistake, that was all. Wait . . . Might it be that he had an unlisted number? But wouldn't the operator have told her that? "As I was waiting for an answer, the line went dead very suddenly," she said.

"Oh, hell!" Jim exclaimed. "No electricity and now no phone." Then in a lighter tone, "But we do have butane to cook with, candles for light, plenty of food and liquor. And—" His eyes circled the table, "we have each other. What more do we need?"

Vickie's glance turned toward Anita and she saw the adoration evident in the girl's face as she looked at this man who spoke. Norman's attention, however, was on her, and sensing this, she turned her eyes his way. Here she read the perplexity and interest that was always in his expression. He was curious about her. Why? It was beginning to annoy her a little, and beneath it all lurked a fear that she did not care to admit, a fear of him that was unreasonable, a distrust that she could not quite understand.

Then out came the words that she had been withholding. "My door opened quite suddenly during the night. It—rather startled me to say the least."

Now the expression that appeared on Anita's face made her catch her breath. All the terror she had felt in the night was mirrored in this girl's eyes.

"Oh, Vickie," Jim said. "You should bolt your door at night. Twice we've had prowlers here."

"Prowlers?"

"Hell, yes. You know there's a stairway from the balcony that goes down near the end of the house, back by the garage."

"Oh. But—prowlers in a place as remote as this? I shouldn't think that . . . "

"Of course," Jim said. "In a way—"

Norman interrupted. "Yes, Vickie. Don't you see how the very isolation of this place can be to a criminal's advantage? A crime can be committed, and by the time help arrives out here, the perpetrator can be long gone."

"Burglary is not unheard of in these parts," Jim added.

"Or a murder," Norman said. "The same would apply if the crime were murder instead of burglary or robbery."

A strange silence, heavy and embarrassing followed, and Vickie saw that the three occupants of this house were looking directly at her. Could it be only to avoid one another's eyes? she wondered, or was there a far more sinister reason?

"That's a—disquieting thought," she said, for someone had to break the sudden hush that was so chilling.

"But true," he said. "Very true."

"Knock it off," Jim told him. "Are you trying to scare these girls?"

And Vickie saw a shudder pass through Anita's body, and a painful look of distress cross her face.

"It's interesting when you think about it," Norman continued, disregarding Jim's words, "that a successful murder is one that should be very well planned."

Vickie wondered what he was attempting to do. Couldn't he see how Anita was reacting to this subject? She looked at his face, so placid, so benign. He's speaking all the wrong lines. He's completely out of character. He's not the same person he was last night at all. Why don't you remove yourself from the stage? she wanted to ask. Become the audience again. I liked you better that way.

"Yes," he continued. "Planned precisely with plenty of thought to details." He looked at each of them. "Tell me, haven't any of you ever thought of committing a murder? In a hypothetical sense, of course."

"No," Jim replied quickly, "and I think we'd better talk about something else. Or how about a game of cards? Poker or—"

"Now, Jim, surely at one time or another you have given some thought to murder; you too, Anita, and you, Vickie. Everyone has. It's perfectly natural really and makes for interesting speculation. There is even a game called Murder, you know. At one time it was quite popular, and it takes more thought than poker."

"I have never heard of this game," Anita said uneasily.

"Then it's time you did, Senorita," Norman told her. "Would you like to play, Vickie?"

She felt hot and then cold. These people! Anita's madness, and now this—sadistic, morbid streak becoming evident in Norman. It's this house, this place, this isolation. It must bring out the worst in all of us. From the corner of her eye she saw Jim's body stiffen. "If the rest of you want to play, I'm willing," she said. I seem to be taking Phil's part in this drama, she thought; an understudy replacing him in his jolly good fellow role. Ever obliging. The good sport. I hate it.

"Okay. Why not?" Jim said, with a shrug of his huge shoulders. "It might help pass the time at that, while we wait for this damn wind to stop blowing."

"It is not as fierce as it was," Anita observed. "I think it will be over soon."

Norman rose to his feet. "Shall we go into the living room?" he asked, "and—"

"You three go," she interrupted rather breathlessly. "I—I would not be good at playing the game, and anyway I must wash the dishes."

"Actually we should have at least six to play," Norman said, "but it can be done with four. With only three it is impossible. Come on. You'll find it quite interesting."

"Anita and I will clear the table and join you in a very short time," Vickie told him. "All right?"

"Of course. We'll be waiting for you," he replied and then laughed a little. "Don't look so glum, you three. Who knows? You might enjoy the game."

After he and Jim had gone, Vickie hurriedly began to remove the dishes from the table and forced herself to appear cheerful and enthusiastic, but to no avail. Anita moved slowly as though heavy with dread. In her eyes burned a haunted look of apprehension.

"Norman is an unpredictable person, isn't he?" Vickie asked lightly. "One moment he can be so quiet, and the next he—"

"He brings trouble. Listen!" Anita whispered. "Do you hear?"

Vickie stood quite still hearing nothing but the dying wind; its voice was now becoming a dirge, a death song.

"You were right, Anita. The wind isn't blowing as hard as it was at all. Surely the storm is nearly over."

"No, no. Listen!" Anita stared wide-eyed at Vickie. "Sh! Kathleen is calling. Can you hear her?" she whispered. "She is calling my name."

"Please, Anita! No. You must not say such things, nor think them, either. It's only the wind you hear."

"Anita, Anita," the girl murmured. "That is what it says."

Vickie listened and then froze, for it seemed as if she, too could hear the voice. "Come, let's go. Let's go play Norman's silly game. It might be fun—and we won't be alone."

"She calls from the hills."

Vickie reached for the girl's hand, a hand as cold as death, and led her into the living room where they found a blaze upon the hearth, and new candles lit in the candelabra. She had hoped the draperies would be open, but they were not, and the room was filled with shadows that moved eerily.

"Well! That didn't take long," Norman remarked with surprise as they entered. "What about the KP duties?"

"We didn't finish," Vickie told him. "The dishes can wait."

"Good. Now, one of us must be the detective and wait outside in the hall. When he or she is called into this room there will be a simulated corpse. The sleuth will then question those in here to learn who committed the crime. Since there will be but two of us, this should make it relatively simple. Now, all questions must be answered honestly, and only once is the detective allowed to accuse someone of murder. If he is wrong, he loses, and must be our Sherlock Holmes again. Understand? Ready?"

Anita said nothing as she stared dazedly around the room. Jim remained silent also, as he watched the others.

"Well, I suppose we are," Vickie said hesitantly, with a feeling of dread.

"Okay. Who wants to go first? Who shall be our first brilliant investigator? You, Vickie?" Norman asked.

"Me?" Then she laughed. "I'm not brilliant, but I'll do my best to make you think I am."

As she walked toward the hallway, he said, "And no eavesdropping at the door."

"I beg your pardon," she said with mock dignity as she left the room. Norman closed the carved double doors behind her. She walked to the end of the hall and looked out at the sand-strewn patio. The wind had indeed slackened and the sky was slowly turning from orange to gray as clouds began to gather. The well. Always her eyes were drawn to it and as she watched, fascinated, she saw the bucket swinging slowly, deliberately, as though an unseen hand pushed it gently to and fro.

"Vickie?" It was Norman's voice she heard.

"I'm here."

"Come in. We're ready for you," he called.

She entered the room, and though she knew this was only a game, the sight of Anita, lying face down on the floor near the fireplace, was startling and she stopped abruptly.

"There's the victim. Who was the cause of this beautiful girl's untimely death?" Norman asked.

"This is a rather grisly game, isn't it," she remarked.

There was no reply to her words, but she did not miss the dark frown on Jim's face, and the serious expression Norman wore. Slowly she approached Anita, and then looked at the area around her. The poker was not in its proper place, but had been left propped against the fireplace instead of being with the small shovel and broom. She pointed toward it, and looked at Norman. "Is this the murder weapon?" she asked.

"It is."

He was standing near the piano. Jim was seated at the bar. Both men were of equal distance from the "victim."

A motive, she thought. Which would have a motive? Then an interesting thought crept into her mind. She had observed how displeased Norman was with Jim's attention to this girl, and even to herself. The death of Kathleen was close to him still. If he knew of the relationship between Anita and Jim. . . . She took a deep breath and was a bit shocked at the turn her thoughts had taken. After all, this was only a game they were playing. Although Anita was motionless she was very much alive—wasn't she? She shivered and looked at Norman, wondering if he harbored a vindictive nature, a consuming desire for revenge.

"Did you have a reason for wanting this girl dead?" she asked him.

His eyes flickered for a second, or was it the fire, or the glow from the candlelight that produced this effect? She saw him glance at the figure on the floor. "Yes," he replied.

She was taken aback. The game seemed too real and far too disturbing. She could look at this tall, handsome man no longer. Her eyes went to the dark and gloomy countenance of Jim Burant. "Were you involved in the death of this girl?" she asked.

For a long moment he did not reply, and the expression in his eyes was one of anger. Then in a low voice he said, "Yes."

"Oh," she murmured. "You were involved, and you, Norman . . . " She held her breath. What had she asked him? Only if he had a reason for wanting Anita dead. And he had answered in the affirmative. She felt her cheeks flush. How awful of her to phrase the question in this way, and how dreadful of him to answer as he had!

Then she laughed nervously. "I—Uh, I understand now why you both answered my questions as you did. I mean, you were both implicated, because the girl had to be murdered in order to play the game. That makes me as guilty as you two." She breathed again and with relief. For a fleeting moment she thought of how pleased Phil would be at the way she had extricated herself from this faux pas, or had she?

"That's right," Norman said, and mentally she blessed him.

Now she again looked at the poker, then walked over to Jim. "May I see your hands?" she asked.

His eyebrows raised as he complied, and slowly she ran a finger across his palms. She found the faintest smudge, but this, she knew, might be only circumstantial evidence. No doubt he had built the fire. Now she crossed the room to where Norman stood, and immediately he extended his hands for inspection. There was no dark streak. However, he may have brushed it off. She would take a chance, and turning back toward Jim she said, "You are the murderer," and the words seem to hang in midair.

A strange tingling went through her body as the coldest breath of air she had ever felt wrapped itself around her, enveloping her, and causing her to move hurriedly toward the hearth and the warmth of the blaze upon it. Norman and Jim were looking at her uncertainly, and she felt like a fool. How absurd to let this game unnerve her so! "I—I suddenly felt—cold," she explained. "Nerves, I suppose. Silly."

They did not reply, and Anita was rising to her feet, her face pale, her lips trembling. Then Vickie nearly cried out, for nearing them was a swirl of gray smoke. Had it come from the fireplace, she wondered? Was there still enough wind to interfere with the smoke rising from the chimney? If not, then what . . . ?

Now she heard Norman's voice. "Don't be nervous," he was saying, "you made a very sharp detective."

Vickie was backing away from the girl, and moving toward the bar. The vaporous mist still hovered near the place where she had stood. How close it remained to Anita! Then Vickie stared with horror as it began to coil around the girl. Couldn't Jim and Norman see it? Look! She wanted to cry out. Look!

As if from far away she again heard Norman speak. "Okay. Who's to be our next detective? Ladies first? Would you care to have the honor, Anita? You made an excellent corpse; never moved a muscle. Did you notice that, Jim?"

"I don't believe I did," the man answered coldly.

"Well, she was great. Acting is a natural for most women, I've learned. Do you want to be next, Anita?" he asked. "Or would you rather Jim or I left the room?"

"No. I want to leave." Her words were low, measured and she spoke with effort. "I have a headache. I want an aspirin."

"A headache?" Norman asked. "How's that for imagination? You weren't really struck with a poker," he said teasingly.

"Good God!" Vickie murmured under her breath. They don't see—what I see, she told herself. It is only I who can watch this small transparent cloud following Anita across the room. I am mad! I am sick! If I say anything then they will know. She lowered herself into a nearby chair and brushed at the cold, icy moisture covering her brow, and clenched her teeth to keep from screaming a warning at Anita.

She looked at one man's face and then at the other. Obviously they were unaware of anything unnatural, of an eerie presence in the room. Were they watching her? She must appear composed. She must play the part of a sane person, and not lose her hold on reality. If they did not see it then neither did she, not really.

When the door closed behind Anita, the atmosphere of the room changed. Vickie began to feel warm again, alive and real. However, the strange malignancy that was always in this room remained, she noticed. This aura she had felt when they arrived, she and Phil, the day before yesterday, and every time she entered.

"This time you be the corpse," Jim was saying, giving Norman a chilling glance.

Norman nodded. "I'll gladly be the victim," he said, then added in a barely audible tone that only Vickie seemed to hear; "It's not the first time I've been one. Let's think," he said, raising his voice. "How shall I be murdered? Any ideas, Vickie?"

"No. No, I'm afraid not."

"Poison," Jim suggested, icily.

"Excellent. How?" Norman asked.

"A drink, here from the bar."

"Of course. Very good." His voice was calm and quiet.

"Rat poison," Jim said in a tone bordering on vehemence.

There was a pause before Norman answered, and an expression of wariness appeared on his face. He forced a smile. "Who did it? Shall it be you, Vickie? After all, poison has always been a favored method of disposal among women."

"Then that might make it too easy for Anita to solve. I'll be the one," Jim told them.

"If you insist," Norman replied, as he left the piano and sprawled out on a chair. "Now you two must be found an equal distance from me. And, oh yes; now for the evidence. If a glass is near me, that would be too obvious. At the bar! That's it. Place a single glass there with a little something in the bottom; sherry perhaps."

Vickie watched as this was done and then she said, "Jim, I wonder if it would be better for you not to remain at the bar, since you are the—killer." His face blurred before her, and she wished she had not spoken these words. He seemed to be looking at her strangely and thoughtfully with brooding eyes.

"But wait," Norman murmured after a pause. "If he stayed in the same place where he was before, wouldn't it be less noticible than if he moved?"

"You're right," Vickie agreed. "The move might cause suspicion."

But Jim was now before the fireplace where he shook his head obstinately. "I'll stay here. We don't want to make it too difficult for her. However, she probably won't expect me to be guilty twice in succession."

"True—possibly," Norman conceded. "Vickie, would you call her please?"

She walked to the doors, opened them and called Anita, but there was no answer. "I'll get her," she said as she closed the doors and stepped out into the hall. Now she could breathe easier with this barricade between herself and the malice inside that room.

"Anita?" She called again as she looked down the darkened hallway and then crossed to the dining room. From there she entered the kitchen.

"Anita?"

Already the grease had grown gray where the bacon had fried, and the cooking utensils and eggshells remained in the sink. Vickie glanced at this evidence of their hasty departure, and frowned as she recalled the reason for it. Now she became curious about the girl's whereabouts. She opened the door at the far side of the kitchen and found a laundry. Beyond this was a storeroom. These would be directly below Norman's room, she realized. Crossing them, she opened another door that she found led into the garage.

"Anita?"

Then she recalled the girl's wish to take an aspirin. Of course. She must still be in her room. Hurriedly she left the garage and crossed the patio, finding the sand gritty against the flagstone. It made an unpleasant rasping sound beneath her feet. Now that the wind had died, there was a strange stillness in the air. "Anita!" she called to shatter the silence, and knocked firmly on the girl's door. "Are you all right?" But there was no sound from within.

Vickie reached for the door knob. It turned easily in her hand, and she opened the door a few inches. "Anita, are you here? We're ready for you."

There was no response, and a sudden feeling of alarm filled her. She opened the door wider and stepped into a colorful, unoccupied room. Hurrying across it she opened the bathroom door. Anita was not there, and Vickie ran back to the patio, and with a feeling of apprehension turned toward the hills in the distance. "She calls to me," the poor, bedeviled girl had said.

Then she heard the door open that led into the house. Jim stood there. "What's wrong?" he asked, almost laughingly. "Is she hiding from us?"

"I don't know," she replied. "I can't find her. I don't understand."

"You looked inside her room?"

"Well—yes." Now she wondered if she shouldn't have. "I also looked in the kitchen, the laundry, the storeroom and garage."

"Anita!" he shouted, and a cold chill crept down Vickie's spine, as she thought of the voice in the wind.

"Can't you find her?" This was Norman who appeared at the patio door, and his voice revealed his incredultiy. Then he came outside, walked the length of the patio and looked over the far wall. "Anita!" he called

"I'll be damned," Jim said, and reentered the house, only to appear a moment later on the balcony. He walked toward his room and vanished inside.

Vickie saw that Norman was running up the outside stairway, near the garage, and when he reached the balcony, he stared off across the miles of desert stretching in all directions.

Vickie walked toward the gate, wondering if the wind had blown it open or if . . . She stepped through it and circled the wall surrounding the house and calling to the girl again and again. She viewed the wind-scoured, corrugated earth, the world of sharp thorn-bearing plants. It had to be fear that had driven Anita into this hostile and forbidding domain, this land where she could not survive for long.

"I can't see her," she heard Jim call, and looking up saw that he was using binoculars. "I'll get the car and . . . "

"So will I," Norman called back, and Vickie watched as he quickly descended the stairs and opened the garage doors. A moment later, Jim had arrived, stepped into his car and backed it out. Then with a squeal of brakes, he turned the corner of the wall and with a roar drove toward the road.

"Come, Vickie," Norman said as he opened his car door. "I want you to go with me. You can look while I drive."

With a sense of relief she stepped inside, knowing that it would have been unbearable to remain here at the house alone.

From the cloud of dust, they saw that Jim had turned north, so Norman took the road leading southeast. They drove slowly as they searched. "She couldn't have gone far," he said. "There wasn't time."

"I can't understand why she did this," Vickie said because it was the reasonable thing to say. How did she dare speak the truth? How could she tell Norman that it was his dead sister who had driven the girl away—perhaps to her death?

"I hope it wasn't the game we were playing that disturbed her," Norman said. "Sometimes I forget that Anita is—extremely emotional." He looked into the distance where the wind still played, sending small whirlwinds pirouetting across the sand. "Her mother expressed fears for the girl's sanity yesterday, while we were driving to Los Angeles. She told me that Anita hallucinates occasionally." He took a deep breath. "She sees and hears Kathleen."

"How horrible," Vickie said softly, and a spasm hit her stomach. And I? she wondered. Have I, too, seen Kathleen? Have I heard her and felt her presence? "How long has Anita had these—hallucinations?" she asked.

"Her mother first noticed this change in Anita about six months ago."

Six months. When Kathleen died, Vickie was thinking.

"She must not have come in this direction," Norman said. "We would have found her by now, unless she's hiding behind rocks."

He pulled the car to the side of the road and stopped. Then he stepped outside and studied the area over which they had driven. There was a sad expression on his face that made Vickie wonder if he might be thinking of his sister.

"Norman," she said, as she got out of the car, "what was she like?"

He looked at her quizzically.

"I mean Kathleen."

"I rather thought you did. We were both thinking about her, weren't we? She looked so much like you, Vickie. But instead of being as she appeared, and as you are, introspective and romantic, she had another facet. She had a fiery passion, a seething jealousy and a rather vindictive nature as well. She was interesting and Jim was intrigued, but I knew the day she married him she was doomed. Oh, how I tried to persuade her not to go through with it! She was so headstrong, I might as well have been speaking to the wind."

"You were convinced it was not a suitable match?"

He nodded. "I knew the kind of man Jim was—and is. Well, let's turn back. I suppose he's found Anita by now."

Vickie hesitated, and again her gaze traveled over the seemingly endless space, a scene where cactus and rock formations appeared to have been strewn at random by a careless whim of nature.

"Come, Vickie," she heard Norman say. "It's no use. She can't be here. She must have gone in another direction."

And it was at that moment that her eyes caught sight of an unbelievable object. "*Norman!*" she shouted. "*Look!*"

Now she was running toward it across the sand and around brushwood and tumbleweeds, running breathlessly to reach an automobile half submerged, half hidden in the sand. "It's Phil's car!" she cried out incredulously.

He was at her side, and when they reached the cove framed by rocks, he exhaled sharply. "What the hell?"

She stopped, but he quickly approached the half-buried vehicle and pulled open the door.

"I—I'm afraid to look," she moaned. "Oh, God!"

"No one's inside," he called to her.

"But—where is he? Why is his car here? I don't understand."

5

THEN HER EYES widened, showing the horror that gripped her mind. "He tried to come back," she cried. "Oh, Norman, that was what happened! He was on his way to the house and couldn't see because of the storm. He drove in here, here to the poor protection of these rocks and then. . . . "

No longer could she voice her thoughts. Obviously he had left the car, which must have become like a smothering tomb, and attempted to make his way on foot. Suddenly the scene before her blurred, and she felt Norman's arms around her. "Are you all right?" he was asking. "I thought you were going to faint."

"No. I'm—okay, but we must hurry. We have to find him before it's too late." Her voice was bordering on hysteria, and quickly she scanned the desert around them.

"Now, Vickie, think a minute. We know he's not between here and the house, so—"

"You mean you're trying to tell me he wandered off in another direction, lost and blinded by the sandstorm? Oh, what can we do?"

Norman scrambled to the top of the highest rock and from there peered into the distance while she watched as one mesmerized. Kathleen. Anita. Phil. It was incredible. "What do you see?" she called up to him.

"I don't see anyone at all," he replied.

His body must be buried in sand, her mind told her. Phil was dead. He was gone from her forever, and she found herself trembling uncontrollably.

"Vickie," Norman said, as he half-slipped, half-crawled back down the rock, "I want you to listen to me and do as I say. You must remain calm and not go all to pieces about this, because—"

"But, Norman!"

"Vickie, there's something here that isn't right. Something that doesn't add up."

"What do you mean?"

"I can't tell you that, because I'm not sure what it is. But just promise me that you'll not go running off into the desert in an attempt to find him."

"But I insist that we find him. What do you think I am?"

"I think you are a young woman in great danger of losing her life."

"Do you mean by getting lost while trying to find Phil?"

"In a way."

"In a way? What kind of double-talk is that? Someone has to look for him," she snapped indignantly.

"And someone will. Come back to the car. We'll drive to a service station about five miles from here. It's on this road, leading to Palm Springs."

Mystified, Vickie rode beside Norman saying nothing until he spoke again. "I want you to be careful, very careful," he said. "Stay within calling distance of me at all times."

She glanced toward him. Who is this man? she wondered. What strange thoughts are in his mind? "I don't understand," she murmured.

"And that, Vickie, is good." He drove swiftly along the desert road, and rounding a curve she saw ahead a structure that could only be the station. It stood alone in the vastness that surrounded it. "If we're in luck, Pete's phone will not be out of order," Norman said. "Chances are the line has been repaired by now."

She stared ahead saying nothing. It was difficult to curb the tears that could have flowed so easily, and her throat felt constricted as if strong hands were around it. Then there was the fear; never before had she ever felt so alone, so abandoned.

When they reached the station, the door swung open and a small, weathered man stepped toward them. "Oh, it's you," he greeted Norman. "Need some gas?"

"That and some information, Pete. First of all is your phone working?"

The man nodded. "Has been for thirty minutes. Just called the wife in fact. Devil of a storm we had, wasn't it?"

"It certainly was."

"I felt sorry for you yesterday seeing you drive past here on your way to Burant's. No day to drive in, I told myself. You should know better than to drive your car through a sandstorm."

"I do. Did you see me pass here yesterday morning—early?"

"Sure I did; you and that woman who works at the house. She's some looker. I wouldn't miss seeing her. You must have gone a long way."

"Los Angeles."

"That's what I figured. I noticed you didn't bring her back, though. Did she quit?"

"No. She had to stay with her sister who is sick. By any chance did you see Jim Burant go past yesterday morning, toward Palm Springs?"

"That I did. He passed with some other fellow in the car with him. He didn't bring *him* back, either."

"And what about a blue sports car? Did you notice if one went by yesterday toward Palm Springs, or coming from it?"

Vickie held her breath.

"Nope. There was a yellow number with a blonde at the wheel. There was a grey sedan in the morning, about ten. Several station wagons went by during the day and one camper. Wasn't much in that wind!"

"You don't miss much, do you, Pete?"

"Nope. Nothing much else to do but watch the cars and hope they'll stop here. Ever since my wife went to the hospital, that's all I've done. When she's home she can find all kinds of nonsense to keep me busy."

"You're sure that Jim Burant had someone with him when he drove past here yesterday?"

"Certainly. I saw him. A stranger, he was. No one who lives around these parts. I couldn't get a good look at him, of course. Burant was driving too fast. I saw that he had light hair, though. You know, light brown."

"I'll use the phone now, Pete. I want to call the highway patrol. There may be someone missing on the desert."

"Missing? Who?" the man asked suddenly. Here was an event of interest in his usually dull day.

"Anita, the girl working for Burant. She probably just went for a walk, but we have become a little concerned."

Vickie looked questioningly toward Norman as he walked inside the station. Why had he not mentioned Phil? Why was he avoiding it.

"Are you visiting at Burant's house?" the man asked, looking in the window and grinning at her.

"Yes," she replied.

"Nice place."

"Very attractive. Are you positive that you saw no blue sports car pass here yesterday or this morning?"

"Never did," he insisted.

"But one could have passed during the night," she said.

"Not likely. No one but a fool would have driven this road last night during that sandstorm. If a car coming from Palm Springs came along here, I think I would have seen it, because the lights would shine right in my eyes. I didn't sleep good last night; the wind kept banging that metal sign over there. What a racket!"

Norman came out of the station, paid for the gasoline, and turned the car back toward the house. "The search will begin immediately," he told her, "for Anita."

"And what about Phil?" she cried.

"I said nothing about him or his car. They'll spot that in a hurry, and will begin to look for the driver."

"This is insane! I can't understand why you didn't—"

"The reason is a good one. Vickie, I'm going to need your trust and cooperation. When we get back to the house say nothing about what we found, or what we fear. Promise?"

"Then tell me why Phil didn't drive his car to Palm Springs, and why Jim said it was parked at the airport there. Why was it left where it was? Why did Phil ride with Jim? Wait! I wonder if something went wrong with the motor, and—but no. There would have been no reason Jim couldn't have told me that."

Norman glanced toward her then back at the road.

"Well, is there?" she asked.

"There's a very good reason, Vickie."

"Then I demand to know what it is."

He looked back at her, this time uncertainly, but he did not reply. And now the pent up tears began to pour down her cheeks. "He killed him!" she sobbed. "Phil is dead and Jim is to blame. All of this—this whole trip has been a ruse of some kind. There is no Barton Lecursi, and probably Jim had no intention of selling his motel at Palm Springs."

Surely she was losing her mind. Surely this entire experience had never really taken place. She was sickened by these thoughts. No wonder it had seemed like a drama to her. It was a dream! Yes, that was it. I'm having a nightmare. "I want to wake up!" she cried out.

Now Norman pulled to the shoulder of the road and stopped the car. "Vickie! Vickie, please," he begged. "Listen to me. You must calm down. I can honestly say I think Phil is alive. I feel you're mistaken about what has happened to him. You must stop crying. We can't let Jim see you like this, or he'll know that we found the car."

"And why shouldn't he know?"

"I just don't want him to learn it from us. He'll find out soon enough from the police, and I want to see his face when he does. His reaction is most important to me."

"Why do you have to be so damn mysterious?" she cried angrily. "You've behaved in such a strange manner ever since we arrived. What is it with you? What is your reason for coming to the desert? You're not here to rest; that was a lie. There is a far different reason for your presence in Jim's house. Anita said something about your bringing trouble with you."

He nodded. "She's right, and so are you. It wasn't a need for rest that brought me here. That was a lie. And I suppose my behavior has been puzzling; I have a puzzling problem to solve. And frankly I've been damned bewildered about you and your husband, and the real reason you are here."

"The real reason?" she cried. "Have you been deaf? You know Phil is trying to negotiate a sale between Jim and this—Lecursi. If there is such a person," she added hesitantly, as she brushed away her tears.

"Do you have a reason to doubt his existence?" Norman asked with interest.

"I tried to phone him. No person by that name is listed."

"This doesn't surprise me. Jim doesn't own a motel in Palm Springs, either, and never did."

"*What?*"

"Vickie, I want to trust you with some more information. I may be a fool to do this, but—I like you, and I . . . " He looked at her closely. "Will you promise to tell no one what I am about to say?"

She stared at him, stunned.

"Are you lying to me now?" she inquired coldly. "Who is my enemy? You or Jim?"

His face darkened and he turned from her.

"Oh, please," she begged tremulously. "I'm sorry. Forgive me. But surely you are mistaken. There has to be that motel, it's the reason Phil and I came here."

"Vickie, Vickie. Perhaps it wasn't the reason. Actually, I'm not sure why you're at Jim's house. Of course, it's not impossible that your husband thought Jim had one that he was interested in selling."

"I know he did."

"I'm not that positive."

She shivered. What did he mean? She looked at him quizzically. "You—you wanted to tell me something?" she asked.

"The question is, do I dare? Do you trust me? Will you give me your promise not to reveal to Jim what I want to say? Can there be mutual trust between us?"

She took a deep breath. "There has to be," she said. "I promise." She looked from his face then, not wanting him to detect the doubt that must show in her eyes.

"Well, first of all my taking Anita's mother to Los Angeles yesterday was not because her sister is ill. The woman is quite well. It was her husband we went to see."

Then Norman had lied about that, also, Vickie was thinking.

"The man is with the police department there, and has been unearthing some very important information for me. What I learned does not directly concern you, except for one very important factor. This brings us back to what I said earlier. There's a possibility that your life is in danger."

He was mad, she decided. He, too, had somehow been brought under the spell of that house, that evil, eerie something that hovered there.

"Just be cautious," he was saying.

"And of course, you won't tell me why."

"Not yet, Vickie. I have to be sure about something first."

"And what is that?"

"It concerns my sister."

"Kathleen?"

"Yes. And that is what brought me here."

"I can only suppose there is a question in your mind about her death."

"There is. Running off the way she did was suicidal. This was an action contrary to her personality. In spite of her fragile appearance, she was a fighter, not a quitter."

"Then you think . . . " Vickie saw again the open friendly face of Jim Burant. He could not—and yet, hadn't she accused him of murdering Phil? Hadn't this gone through her mind and poured out in hysterical words only a short time ago?

"And then there is Anita, and what she sees."

Vickie's eyes widened. Did Norman believe that his sister's spirit remained in the house?

"Her mother wrote to me soon after Kathleen's death, telling me about her daughter's—problem. At first I disregarded what Anita thought she saw and heard as the imagination of a girl who had been shocked by my sister's death, a girl who lived out here in an isolated spot with too little to do—a victim of an empty life. However, after a while I began to wonder if she was seeing—imagining that she saw what she did, because of a guilty conscience. As soon as I was able to get away, I came to the Desert Flower to observe. The trip brought about quite a disclosure."

"Norman! Do you believe that Kathleen was—"

"Murdered," he said, and the air seemed to become freezing with the icy hatred and anger in his voice. "And now I'm closing in, Vickie. The reason we played the game we did this morning was not to while away the time."

"I didn't think it was," she murmured.

"Neither did Anita and Jim," he said. "They knew."

"And that's why she ran away?"

"Of course. She and Jim have been on intimate terms for a long time. Kathleen discovered this, and . . . I have one thing left to learn. How did they bring about my sister's death?"

"Anita told me, Norman, that Jim was in Los Angeles when it occurred."

"He was. In fact, we had dinner together the night of the fifteenth. He was there on business, he said, something regarding the purchase of an apartment house in Northern California near San Francisco."

"San Francisco?"

"Think," he told her. "Try to remember if Phil was away on a trip last August—the middle of the month."

"Why—yes. Yes, I recall it well. I wanted to go with him, but he said he would be so busy, and the weather, of course, would be searing. I hate heat, and the subject was dropped. I seldom accompany him on his trips, actually. My shop keeps me busy, and . . . But Norman, Phil couldn't have been involved in that transaction with Jim. The trip here was the first time they met."

"But was it, Vickie?"

"What do you mean?"

"What I learned yesterday was of tremendous interest. Jim had a good alibi. Not only did he have dinner with me, but he had checked in at the Hilton where he spent a great deal of time speaking with another guest—a Philip Bishop from San Francisco."

She gasped. "Norman! No!"

"I have wondered why Jim was not notified of Kathleen's disappearance. Yesterday I learned that he had left word here, that he would be staying at the International Hotel. When the authorities tried to contact him there, they discovered he had never checked in. By the time they found he had stayed at the Hilton, he had already checked out. However, since there was no reason to connect him with the death of his wife, the matter was not pursued. You can't arrest a man for changing his mind about the hotel where he is to stay.

"According to Anita's mother, Jim's car left his house at eight o'clock that Saturday morning when Kathleen vanished. She is certain of this. However, I have since learned that Pete saw Jim's car race past his station that morning at nine-thirty. Why would it take him an hour and a half to drive nine miles? Vickie, I've been half out of my mind thinking of what must have taken place. He drove Kathleen out there on the desert and left her. In my book that amounts to murder."

"Oh, God," Vickie murmured. "Surely he didn't do that."

"Pete lives at that station and doesn't miss a thing that passes by. This is his life."

"And Anita's mother? Could she have been mistaken about the time?"

"No. She wasn't feeling well that morning, and took some medication that was not to be repeated until after four hours, so she looked at the clock, jotted down the time when she took the first dose and heard the car back out of the garage."

"Why has she been telling you things that might possibly involve and even incriminate her own daughter?"

"She doesn't know this. She doesn't realize what I suspect."

In Norman's voice was both bitterness and pity.

"Then her only reason for writing to you about Anita's— hallucinations, was her concern for the girl's mental health?"

"That was all. Helen likes me and wanted my advice. Whenever I visited here, she was always friendly. While she has never spoken of it, I felt that she was not fond of Jim." After a moment he added, "Little did she know that it was her daughter's belief in ghosts that started the wheels in my head spinning."

"Norman, do you—do you believe in such things?"

"What? Ghosts? Hell, no! Vickie, surely you don't."

"Of course not."

"Anita is sick."

"I know that."

"Well, we'd better get back to the house. She is probably there by now. I have a strong feeling that Jim will find *this* girl before it's too late."

"Norman, why didn't Anita's mother—did you say her name was Helen? Why didn't she return with you?"

"She needed to see her doctor; x-rays etcetera."

Vickie stared at the house in the distance, but in her mind loomed the image of the man she had married. Why had he pretended that Jim was a stranger to him? How did he fit into the picture of ugliness and hatred surrounding them? Where was he now? Phil, oh, Phil, she thought, why have you done this to me?

As they drove through the iron gates that still stood open, they saw Jim's car approaching from a trail-like road to the west. They pulled up before the house, stepped from the car and watched as he entered the driveway. He was alone.

"You didn't find her either?" he called to them.

"No," Norman replied, "so I called the highway patrol from Pete's."

"Good."

Vickie searched his face as he walked toward them. He was frowning and appeared more angry than worried.

"I've looked everywhere," Jim said. "That crazy kid is hiding. I'm not looking for her anymore. When she gets hungry she'll show up."

They entered the house and he walked directly to the bar. "What a hell of a morning this has been! Let's have a drink."

"No thank you," Vickie said, as he turned toward her, and she saw the surprise in his face.

"Have you been crying? Forget it. Don't worry about Anita. She's okay wherever she is. That one can take care of herself."

"I hope so," she said.

"Believe me, I know," he told her. "Don't waste your tears. It's not all that bad. We'll be seeing her again before this day is over. She likes to run off and pout. Have a drink, then we'll rustle up some food. After that we'll all feel better."

"Food?" Vickie sank down upon the sofa, feeling a little sick. "The kitchen is a mess. I'll take care of it in a minute."

"You'll do nothing of the kind. You're my guest." Then he startled her by a little laugh. How could anyone feel mirth at a time like this, she wondered?

"I was just thinking," he said, "that here might be the reason Anita took a powder. She didn't want to clean up the kitchen."

"I don't feel that such a remark at this time is humorous," Norman remarked coldly. "She could be in the same trouble in which Kathleen found herself."

"Norm!" Jim exclaimed. "That girl wasn't out of our sight ten minutes when she vanished. Obviously she is hiding somewhere. Has anyone looked in the storage room? If you want to know the truth, that damn game scared her. Didn't you see the look on her face? Come on, give me a hand in the kitchen. And Vickie, you stay here."

After the men left the room, Vickie leaned back against the cushions and thought of how right she had been about this house, about their coming here, about the atmosphere of rancor, bitterness and malevolence. She should have listened to her instincts that warned her out of this place. She had followed Phil, and now he was gone from her. Tears again filled her eyes. Even if he returned, she would never feel the same. He had deceived her, closed a door between them. She could never be part of his life. How little she must really know of his activities! How she had wanted his love, longed to be close to him. But now, suddenly it no longer seemed to matter.

She put the drink aside and rose to her feet. She would go to her room and freshen up a little, then she would help prepare lunch. As she walked through the hallway, she lifted the receiver of the telephone and heard the dial tone. It was no longer out of order, however she knew she would make no attempt to call Phil again—ever. Walking toward the stairway, she paused, then stepped out into the

patio. Kathleen's oasis. Yes, Vickie thought, it did appear
to be one. She fingered a palm frond, and saw how the
wind had damaged the tree. Several chairs were over-
turned, and one small table was on its side. Only the well
was invincible, and as she neared it, she somehow felt very
close to the woman who had been Kathleen. They had
something in common—a love denied.

She stood beside it, then cautiously looked over her
shoulder; she had not forgotten the pressure she had felt
here only yesterday. No one was near; no one she could
see. She was very much alone, she told herself, but hesitantly she leaned over to look into the water wondering all
the while if it would be her own reflection that would gaze
back up at her, or the face she had seen before. Vickie
knew that somewhere in her mind was the desire to see
Kathleen again, to see that someone who had appeared in
the wind outside her door. It would help, she felt to know
the truth, and this seemed the only way. Was the presence
of Kathleen here, or not? Was there a phantom, or was she
having hallucinations?

Did she believe in ghosts? Norman had wanted to know,
and her answer had been a lie, hadn't it? She was not sure.
She no longer knew what to believe or disbelieve, but her
deep curiosity was becoming a compulsive thing; she could
not resist peering into the darkness of the well. Then suddenly it seemed as if the entire desert screamed. Was the
voice her own? Yes! Yes! It was she who screamed again
and again, for the face staring up at her was that of Anita!

6

SHE WAS LYING on the sofa and Norman was speaking softly. "You're all right, Vickie. You're all right." She attempted to sit up, but he placed his hand against her shoulder and she felt her head resting again on a cushion. "You fainted, but you're doing fine now."

"That's not true. I have never fainted in my life. Oh! Norman, I—I saw something. I really did. I saw . . . "

He nodded as though he knew—almost as if he, too, had looked into the well, and. . . . Then the realization hit her. It had not been something supernatural. Anita really had been in the well!

"Oh, no!" she cried. "Norman, is Anita . . . ?"

He nodded again. "But don't let it affect you like this. You've had a shock, I know. But now you must try to recover. It's a bad experience that you'll have to erase from your mind quickly."

"Oh, my God!"

"Here, drink this." And she opened her eyes again to see Jim standing there, a glass in his hand.

"I don't want it."

"I don't care if you want it or not. Drink it."

She looked again at his face and saw an expression of anger mixed with grief.

This time when she sat up Norman did not attempt to restrain her. She felt the glass in her hand and sipped the brandy.

"Here's Pete now," she heard Jim say, as a car door was slammed. And he hurried from the room.

"Pete?" she asked, bewildered.

Norman nodded. "He's bringing a winch," he told her.

"A winch? Oh. Oh, yes." Then she pictured what was to be done. "Norman, could it be that all the time we were looking for Anita, she was here—in the —well?"

"I'm afraid so."

She shuddered. "Good Lord, Norman! Why didn't we think to look there first? We were in the patio. I walked right past the well, when all the time she . . . How horrible!"

"Damn it, Vickie. It never occurred to me—to us that she would . . . I still can't understand. I could see her running away from the house because of her insane fears. I could picture her hiding, as Jim said. But to . . . It's incredible."

"I have the feeling that she didn't do it—intentionally," Vickie said in a hushed tone.

"What do you mean?"

The expression on his face silenced her. She shook her

head, and looked toward the fireplace, not wanting to put her thoughts, her own fears into words.

"Vickie, I'll be back in a few minutes. Jim and Pete may need my help. Okay?"

"Yes. Yes, of course," and she again sipped the brandy. The warmth reached her fingers and toes, and what had been the beginning of a tumult within her was starting to subside. She took a deep breath. Perhaps Phil would return and tomorrow they would fly home. She would bury herself in her work and forget. Yes, she must forget. "Phil, please," she murmured. "Please call me."

Her eyes widened with surprise. The telephone was ringing! It must be Phil. He was calling here. He was! The ringing stopped. Someone had answered. She listened. The glass in her hand was shaking, so she put it on the table and stood. It seemed as though her very heart trembled as she waited for the summons to the phone. A summons that did not come. Resolutely she walked toward the hallway, wondering if it might have been from the police in San Francisco. She must know if the man she married was alive or dead. She must know if he was at home or out there somewhere—out there—a lone figure in a stark landscape.

Slowly she opened the doors and saw Norman at the telephone desk. His voice was low and soothing, consoling. His face was pale, and his eyes, as he looked toward her seemed distressed.

Bewildered she turned away. Obviously the call had not been for her. She returned to the sofa and sat down again wondering what the future held, and she felt a desperate kind of cold loneliness sweep through her.

Now the wailing of sirens could be heard. Police? The highway patrol? Of course the authorities would have been notified of Anita's death; since it occurred the way it did there would be questions, many questions.

She reached for the brandy glass and cupped her hands

around it. And she listened as the screaming vehicles came nearer and nearer. How eerie was the sound! Norman had called them to look for the missing girl, but it had been she, Vickie, who had found her. Would she ever forget that upturned face in the dark water of the well? And Phil? A curious thought troubled her. Was it to be she, also, who would find him?

Now the sirens had stopped and she walked to the windows to look outside. A patrol car was parked, and close behind stood an ambulance. She hurried to the living room doors and closed them, not wanting to see, not wanting to hear what was to follow. Since she had been the one to find Anita, they would come here, these men in uniform, and talk to her. No doubt she would learn if they had discovered Phil's car—or if they had possibly found him. All she could do now was wait; just sit and wonder and wait.

It seemed an eternity before the ambulance drove away, and then the doors opened. She looked around to find Jim standing there. "Are you okay, Vickie?" he asked.

"I think so."

"It was a hell of a thing for you, I know."

"It was worse for her—Anita."

He frowned and walked toward her. "She was a sweet kid," he said. "I can't believe she's gone. I just can't. She meant so much. I think I—loved her."

She looked at him. There seemed to be nothing to say.

He sat down on a chair opposite her. The expression on his face now seemed guarded. "I have something to tell you, Vickie, but I don't want it to worry you."

"What is it?" she asked, but knowing what he was about to say.

"We have just learned that Phil's car was found off the road not far from here."

She stared at him. He seemed completely unmoved by

the words he had spoken. Now she must play the part of
the very surprised, shocked wife. It was an effort. She did
not feel up to this deception. "What did you say?" she
cried, thinking how well it had sounded. "Phil's car! Are
you sure?" She was speaking her lines expertly. What had
Norman said about women being actresses? "But
why . . . " She had even managed a gasp, but inside she
felt sick.

"Now, Vickie. Please don't get excited about this. There
is a logical explanation, of course. Apparently the car was
stolen and then abandoned alongside the road. It happens
all the time."

How glibly you lie, she thought. "But are you sure that's
what happened? Do the patrolmen think this?"

"Vickie, please. What else could it have been? That car,
from what they said, was out there all night. No question
about it. The paint is scoured, the glass pitted and it's half
covered with sand. Also there's hardly any gas left in the
tank. I suppose some kids drove it until it went dry. That's
the usual procedure. We'll call Phil and break the news.
Also, we'll pick him up at the airport, of course. I wonder if
he is going to fly back tonight or tomorrow?"

"You didn't answer my question, Jim. Do the patrolmen
think that the car was stolen?"

"Well, they—" His eyes avoided hers.

"Do they discount the possibility that he tried to drive
back here and never made it?"

"Now, Vickie. Don't start imagining things. He would
have hardly done that."

"What do they think?" She persisted.

He shrugged. "Naturally they have considered that. But
it's so unlikely. We know he went to San Francisco and
didn't plan on coming back here until tonight at the very
earliest."

"Did you see him board the plane?" she asked.

He looked at her with surprise. "Well, I didn't actually see him get on it, but there's no reason to think he didn't."

"Except his car," she said, no longer pretending, "and the fact that I have not been able to reach him at our apartment."

She looked at him closely. How clever he was! His eyes now didn't waver from hers for an instant. She wondered how he would react if she told him that he had been seen driving with Phil in his car toward Palm Springs. That Phil's car had never been at the airport. That it was not waiting for Phil's return as he had told her. That he was lying now and had lied before.

There were footsteps in the hall, and he rose to his feet. "The ambulance and patrolmen came from Yucca Valley," he said to her. "I think that—"

Norman and a uniformed man entered the room. Vickie took a deep breath and answered the latter's questions tersely. Yes, she had been the one who found Anita's body. No, the girl had given her no reason to think she might have suicidal tendencies. Yes, the three of them had left the house simultaneously to search for her. No one had remained behind. Yes, they had all returned almost at the same moment.

And then: No, she had not spoken with her husband since he left Palm Springs where he had called her from the airport. Yes, she had tried to reach him in San Francisco, but unsuccessfully. No, she could not think of any reason he would abandon his car. She did not know how much gas remained in the tank when they arrived here. "I am very concerned," she told the officer. "I'm—I am afraid something dreadful has happened to him."

Then he was gone, and Norman told her to stay where she was. He would be back soon with something to eat. And again she was waiting, trying to untangle the thoughts that seemed to be turning and twisting in her mind. After a while he entered the room again, this time with sandwiches and steaming coffee.

"Jim's still in the kitchen," he told her. "He doesn't feel like eating, but he is cleaning up the mess from breakfast. How did things go when he told you about Phil's car being found?"

"I pretended to be very surprised. Of course he could see how puzzled and worried I am."

"Of course."

"Has he tried to call Phil yet? He said he was going to."

"He has tried, but there was no answer. The police in San Francisco will find him if he's there. The search is really rolling, Vickie. The patrolmen here have found nothing to indicate that he is out there." She saw him nod toward the desert. "Nothing is there but his car and a small camper parked somewhere nearby. They checked that out, of course. He isn't in it."

Even the thought of food repulsed her but she decided to make an effort to eat something. "But, I've learned something else," she heard him say, and she looked at him questioningly. Obviously, from his tone of voice he was reluctant to disclose this new information.

"It's something bad, isn't it? What you've learned is bad."

"It could be, but let's not cross bridges. Don't forget, your husband had a reason for concealing the fact that he knew Jim before this visit. Also, he had a purpose for coming here and bringing you with him. We don't know the motive, but in all probability there was something going on that was not, shall we say, on the level? They were working together, and I believe still are, on—God knows what."

"You're trying to tell me that Jim and Phil are mixed up in some kind of a criminal act?" She shivered as she felt a cold sinister numbness beginning to engulf her. Surely Phil

had not been involved in Kathleen's death. It was inconceivable.

He shrugged. "I want you to know that there was no
Philip Bishop on any passenger lists of planes leaving the
airport at Palm Springs yesterday."

She gasped. "That can't be true!"

"According to the authorities it is."

"Ohhhh—that can mean only one thing. He must
be . . . " Her voice was quavering.

"Vickie, I think your husband is very much alive. I
believe he left using an assumed name."

"But, Norman, why?"

He shook his head. "And there's something else. When I
was driving Helen to Los Angeles yesterday, she accident-
ly made a remark, a slip of the tongue. She tried to cover
it, and I saw fear in her eyes. But I learned something you
should know. It's the reason I told you that I think you are
mistaken about what happened to your husband."

"What is it?"

"First I must have your promise that you will never tell
Jim what I'm going to say."

"I'm sick of all this pretense," she cried.

"I know, but it's vital that you carry on with it a little
longer."

"Vital to whom? Norman, I can believe that Jim might
have caused your sister's death, but not that Phil was in
any way implicated."

"Do you want to hear what I found out from Helen?"

"Of course." Now she wondered if his physical appeal
were influencing her; if she had become so hungry for
attention that she was letting him bend her will, her thinking, her hopes. "And I promise not to repeat what you tell
me."

"Phil has visited this house before," he said.

The statement hit her like a blast.

"What!"

He took her hand. "I'm sorry, Vickie, but it's true. And all kinds of thoughts have been going through my mind. I've even wondered if your husband came back here this time to blackmail Jim."

"Norman!"

"It seems improbable, however, that a man coming here with such intentions would bring his wife along. Vickie, did he seem at all reluctant about your coming here?"

"No," she replied hesitantly, recalling how Phil had been the one to suggest she accompany him. Usually this was not the case, and now this thought worried and puzzled her.

"Well," Norman said, "there's little point in our trying to arrive at any conclusions at the moment. The desert will be combed. If Phil is out there, he will be found—and soon. Eat, Vickie, then go to your room and try to rest. I want to take you with me when I go to pick up Helen—if I go."

"Oh, Norman! You've called her then. That poor woman. How did she take the ghastly news?"

"The way you'd expect. It was horrible. She called here to talk to Anita, and . . . I was speaking to her when you came to the door and looked at me. Remember?"

"Oh. Oh, yes. I thought it might be Phil who was calling." She shook her head. "That would be terrible to call one's daughter, only to learn that she had just drowned."

"For a minute I thought she was going to have a heart attack. You can well imagine what a shock it was to her. When I hung up I think she was numb. It was difficult to understand what she was saying. And she was crying, of course. Anyway, she felt that her brother-in-law would either drive her here, or arrange for a flight to Yucca Valley. That wouldn't be nearly as far to go to pick her up as Palm Springs. If she flies she'll call me from the airport."

Norman stared into space now, and after a moment he

said, "Vickie, I feel as if I'm responsible for Anita's death. Indirectly, of course, but if it had not been for me, she and her mother would never have been here."

"Really?"

He nodded. "Did Anita tell you anything about herself and her mother?"

"No, not much," she said, recalling the girl's sad words.

"Well, Helen is not of Mexican descent. Her last name was Logan and she lived in San Diego where she met Juan Pomares. They were married, and she worked in a small restaurant that he managed. Two years later Anita was born, and I think she was only three years old when Pomares decided to move his wife and child to Mexico City and go into business there with an uncle of his. The venture must not have been exactly lucrative, because after he died, Helen and Anita, who was then nineteen, moved back here with little money. I found them working in one of my restaurants. Helen made an attractive hostess. and Anita was working as a waitress. However, they had lived such a quiet, secluded life in Mexico, that they were not at all happy being in such close contact with the public. It wasn't working out, and that's when I thought of Kathleen and Jim, this house, and their current need for help, which is hard to get in such a place as this. But what a fatal mistake I made suggesting they hire Helen and her daughter! Hell! I knew Jim's weakness for women. I just didn't have my mind on what I was doing; I was too involved in other things. But believe me, I've done plenty of thinking about it since."

"You shouldn't blame yourself," she told him. "What has happened was no fault of yours."

"What I did, Vickie, brought death to Kathleen and Anita."

"How could you have possibly known that tragedy would come from the arrangement? You were only trying to help."

He shook his head.

"Norman, I only had a brief glimpse of Helen. She is pretty. Do you think there was anything between her and Jim?"

"No, I really don't. Actually I felt that she didn't like him. I've wondered if this could be because she suspected what was taking place between him and Anita. I wish she had told me, confided in me, then things might have turned out much differently."

"It's futile to look back and regret," she said.

"I suppose so, thank you, Vickie. Right now I have to think about facing Helen. She's such a fine, sensitive person. Anita meant so much to her. She was all she had except for her sister, it seems.

"If I have to pick her up at the airport, I want you to go with me. I don't intend to leave you here alone, as I told you."

"With Jim, you mean."

"Finish eating."

"Sometimes I think, Norman, that you really believe Jim would harm me. How can you consider such a possibility when there is no reason for it?" She noticed she was whispering, and there was a note of uncertainty in her voice.

"Frankly I don't know," he admitted. "It's just that I want to take no chances of having something happen to you."

Their eyes met, then without another word he left the room. As she ate she wondered about what he had told her—everything he had said to her from the time they first met. The lies. The truths. Which were which? And now her throat seemed so constricted that eating was an effort. She drank a cup of coffee, then did as he had told her to do. She went to her room.

7

SHE HAD INTENTIONALLY not glanced toward the well, and as she closed the door behind her she wondered if she ever would again. Now she stood before the dresser mirror staring at herself, shocked at her appearance. She looked positively haggard. Reaching for a brush she used it on her hair until the red in it shone. Then she applied some lipstick and studied her face once more. She sighed. Perhaps nothing would diminish the look of horror that was there, for it was in her eyes. She lay back on her bed and let them close, but only for a second. Anita's face had appeared before her. It was going to take time to erase this from her mind. If she could only go home, she thought.

But how could she, not knowing where Phil was? She must wait. She must stay here and wait. But how much longer?

Looking toward the closet she saw his suitcase, and hanging above it was his suit, the blue one that he had never really liked. It was the brown tweed that he was wearing, she realized. Then she frowned. This would make him more difficult to find. It would blend with the sand and desert growths. Suddenly tears sprung into her eyes.

Why did she cry about him, she wondered. Were the tears for what might have been? How futile! She should weep with anger for the way he had deceived her. For some reason, one for which she had to learn the truth, he had wanted her to think he did not know Jim Burant at all. And what about the nonexistent Barton Lecursi and the motel in Palm Springs? Why had Phil kept his previous visit here a secret?

The tears of fury that sprung into her eyes now were hot, burning hot. If it were not for Norman, she thought, she would have been unaware of . . . She reached for a tissue and wiped away the tears, and for some time she thought of this man, and then a strange kind of doubt began to eat at her. He had lied about the reason for taking Helen to Los Angeles. Was he one who lied often and with ease? Slowly she rose to a sitting position and looked at her reflection again in the dresser mirror.

Vulnerable, Norman had called her. What about gullible? "Oh, Vickie," she mumbled. "You're thinking like a fool." But was she? Doubt like a wave of dark water flowed into her mind. How did she know Phil had been here before? Norman had told her. How did she know Phil and Jim had met in Los Angeles six months ago? Norman again. And it was he who said Jim didn't own a motel in Palm Springs.

And what about Barton Lecursi? Maybe he did have an unlisted telephone number, she told herself. Perhaps San

Francisco is not his home. He might live in the suburbs. Her heart beat faster and faster.

Oh, God! she thought, could it be Norman who had deceived her instead of Phil? It wasn't right that he hadn't reported Phil's car being found in the sand. This still bothered her. She shouldn't have let him get away with that. She had been gullible, stupid and blind, believing him implicitly.

But there was Pete. He had told them he had seen someone riding with Jim. But wait. Had he really seen a passenger in Jim's car? Who was he, this grinning man at the service station? And thinking back, Vickie tried to recall the conversation that took place there. Hadn't something been a little strange about it? It seemed to her now that at the time she had been vaguely conscious of this, but she had been so worried, and shocked that the feeling had been only an illusive, wispy kind of thought. But the words like an echo came back to her.

"Did you see me pass here yesterday morning—early?" Norman had asked.

"Sure I did; you and the woman who works at the house."

"By any chance did you see Jim Burant go past yesterday morning?"

"That I did. He passed with some other fellow in the car with him."

"And what about a blue sports car? Did you notice if one went by yesterday toward Palm Springs, or coming from there?"

"Nope."

"You don't miss much, do you, Pete?"

"Nope. Nothing much else to do but watch the cars and hope they'll stop here."

"You're sure that Jim Burant had someone with him when he drove past yesterday morning?"

"Certainly. I saw him. A stranger, he was . . . "

Vickie's cheeks were aflame. Here was what seemed strange about the conversation. Every question asked had been a leading one, so Pete would not forget the answers that he had been taught to give. Why? Why had the man been instructed to—lie? Money, Vickie decided, knowing well that there are people who will say anything, do anything for a price.

She stood up and ran her hand across her forehead. What was Norman's motive? She shook her head. It was all too puzzling, but without a doubt there was a diabolical scheme that had been adeptly planned and was being cleverly executed. If she could only put the pieces together. And what had they done with Phil? Where was he?

If Pete had lied, then there was but one answer. Phil was out in the desert somewhere. She reached for her sweater, opened the door and looked down to the patio. No one was there. Her eyes circled the balcony. The men must still be in the kitchen. She scurried now past two more rooms and down the outside stairway. She seemed to be trembling all over, her heart hammered against her chest. She would stay close to the wall after going out through the back gate, and surely they would not see her. And then there would be the road. She must avoid that. She would cross it quickly and make her way back toward the place where Phil's car was.

Time was working with her, she decided. Norman wouldn't look for her until he was to leave to pick up Helen, and perhaps there would be no reason to do that. Quite likely her brother-in-law would bring her here in a car.

She stood by the corner of the wall and looked cautiously at the road. The drifted sand had almost obliterated it. If it hadn't been for the tire tracks she would not have been able to follow it with her eyes. Ahead was a grove of ghostly Joshua trees, some of them reaching twenty-five feet into the ashen, sullen sky; a sky that seemed to be sulking after its tantrum. She ran. Here was a chance she was going to have to take. If she reached the trees without being seen, then her escape from the house would be a success.

When she finally stood behind them she caught her breath, startled. Something had scampered near her feet. Then she felt relief as she saw that it was only a lizard who had been disturbed. She waited. There was not a sound from the house. No voice called her name. No car engine was being turned on. She was safe. She had made it, and now she could begin the circuitous route to her destination, peering into the distance for Phil, calling for him. If he could not be found, then Norman had been right, but if he was here, dead or alive, then . . .

If she found him, what would she do? Would she dare return to the house? She could not force herself to go to the service station. But surely she could contact the highway patrol. Once she was far enough away from here she would return to the road, and it would be there that she could get help. She looked behind her toward a rocky crest and now she was running again toward it. How difficult it was to travel quickly through the sand! It seemed to drag at her feet, telling her in a silent way that she was unwelcome in this forbidding wasteland. Suddenly she thought of Kathleen and wondered if she had also felt this way about the overpowering vastness around her, this giant that had eventually dragged the life from her.

Cautiously she forced herself to proceed although the possibility of rattlers and other venomous desert creatures filled her with near paralyzing fear. She thought of Anita and the spider she had described. She also remembered the girl's question. "Do you ever feel the eyes that watch you—watch everything you do?"

Now Vickie peered into the distance knowing that Anita was not referring to arachnids or reptiles. It was another pair of eyes that somehow did seem to be observing every move she made. Vickie, too, could feel them, just as Anita had, and she shivered with the discomfort they evoked.

She walked on, heedful and vigilant, listening for the sound of an automobile. But then, Norman would not have missed her presence yet. He would assume that she was resting in her room.

With this thought a new feeling surged through her, one of strength and freedom as she looked at the endless sky and the miles and miles of earth. It seemed to her as though she were seeing the universe, making everything that troubled her quite small by comparison. A kind of euphoria came over her and she spread her arms wide, palms upward and dismissed from her mind the terrors that this day had brought. No one can hear me, she told herself. No one can touch me and no one can see me but Kathleen. Now she paused and smiled. Upon Vickie's face was a serenity that had been lost these past days.

Now, she realized why Jim liked living here, and what he felt about this vast isolated expanse. Its silence was no longer a thing she felt she must shatter. It was as Phil had said—restful. A large dune rose in front of her. Cautiously, she mounted it.

"No one must see me. No one must find me. No one must know where I am," she whispered. "Not yet."

Reaching the summit, she stealthily stretched out flat and looked around her. The light from the milky sun caught and held the shimmer of metal painted white. It was a camper. Then Vickie recalled Pete's speaking of one passing by his station. Then this much of what he had said was true. She gazed at it and wondered who might be inside; who had left the world of clamor and competition to hide away and absorb the enticing witchery of this place? Well, she would not intrude. She moved away like a shadow, slipping along with trickles of sand to the desert floor again.

Suddenly she was confused. She had lost her sense of direction. Where was the road? Why hadn't she seen it from the mound? Oh, nonsense, she told herself. She couldn't be lost. See, there was the grove of Joshua trees that stood across the road from the house. There it was, far behind her. She had wandered quite a distance, a very long way. But no, no, that was much too far off. It had to be another grove. How difficult it was to find a landmark, for the trees were everywhere! Yesterday these formidable specimens of vegetation had frightened her. Today they shielded her.

She hurried on, not liking the sudden doubt about her location that was creeping into her mind and ruining the calm, drifting sensation of remoteness and seclusion that had been hers just moments ago.

She moved more rapidly now, reminding herself that she was here, not to dream and forget, but to find some trace of her husband. Thoughtfully she gazed at the sky. The sun was not now visible, but it had been to her left, had it not? Yes. She was sure of this, so she should turn and walk in that direction. That should be West

After a while she came upon another trail where cars had passed from time to time. Like the road and the tracks from the trailer, this too, had been a victim of the sand-storm and its direction was barely discernible. She followed it, however, feeling that all trails led somewhere. Soon she paused, and a puzzled expression crossed her face. She had heard something, but was uncertain of what might have caused the noise. There was no wind. Yet it had sounded almost like a sharp whisper of air blowing between rocks, or perhaps among the thorny arms of the Joshuas around her. And then she heard it again. This time it was a sound almost like a voice, one that called to her from somewhere not too far away, and reverberated against the rocks. She stood quite still and listened; every nerve taut. And then it came again. "Vickeeee—Vickeeee."

Spinning around she saw nothing but her own footprints following her. No one was here. She was alone. Surely it was her imagination deceiving her.

She forced herself to walk again, but had not gone far when she stopped dead still.

"Vickeeee—Vickeeee." The wailing echoed once more.

"Phil?" she cried out. "Phil, are you here?"

There was no response and after a moment she moved on chilled with apprehension and bewilderment. It was a madness that filled her very being, she told herself. It was what had bedeviled Anita; Anita who listened to a voice that called her name. She must fight this sickness. She must not listen.

Then, like a soft note from a violin, it came again and she pressed her hands against her ears and attempted to think rationally. It was only because she was alone, she assured herself, alone in such weird, unfamiliar surroundings, that her mind was playing such strange tricks on her.

With this thought she walked on, rapidly now. It had not been real, this human-like sound. And how could she have, even for a moment, wondered if Phil called to her, when all the time what she heard was the voice of a woman. No! she cautioned herself. Not a voice. She had not meant that. It was only a breeze, a singing breeze. She must remember this.

Surely she would arrive at a road soon. Peering into the distance she saw something indistinguishable, vague and ill-defined in the waning light of the late afternoon.

"Vickeeee—Vickeeee."

Her eyes widened with fear. How could she deny that it was a voice? It was louder now and nearer. Much nearer. She ran. Perhaps there was a house at the trail's end. There might be someone there who would help her, a friendly person to whom she could speak. Someone sane to help her fight off this panic and terror that threatened her own sanity.

Then what lay ahead became clearer. She could see a wall, or part of one, for many of the stones had crumbled away. Atop it remained segments of a picket fence. As she approached it she wondered why she saw no house. Had it burned down, perhaps? Then she stopped and stared and knew the reason. Here was not an abode of the living, but a long-forgotten resting place for the dead, where tombstones stood at crazy angles, crosses leaned this way and that, and the weeds grew tall. The trail had led her to a cemetery. To this place the voice had summoned her, and satisfied that she was here, it fell silent and called no longer.

Slowly she walked among the graves where many a protecting fence had been weathered away, leaving only bits of wood lying near the sunken mounds. And she tried to read what was left of the wind-scoured inscriptions.

Abigale Ph . . . Born 1841—Died 18 . . . Jeremiah Peck—Born . . . Died 1878. Here lies . . .

Then something drew her attention to a far corner of the graveyard where a black iron fence enclosed another mound and the tombstone stood erect with a kind of dignity. She approached it with wonder, for this was a recent grave! Incredible as it might seem the headstone read:

Kathleen Corbett Burant
Beloved Wife
1941   1971

8

As though hypnotized, Vickie stood there and stared at the name. Until now Kathleen had been a vision, a young woman not unlike herself, small with golden hair. She had been a phantom in the night, an illusive substance of the day, a misty cloud across the room, a voice that called from the distant hills. She was a silver and blue shadow by the well who looked into its dark depths for water. Kathleen was a will-o'-the-wisp, until now.

The full impact of what had happened to the real, very much alive Kathleen seemed to hit Vickie for the first time. Feeling she had been deceived, she too, had wandered out into the brooding silence and vast expanse of sand and dry vegetation. But it had been summertime and the heat was like a blast from hell, and she . . .

Nearby among the stones and weeds, Vickie saw gray-green plants with small leaves and the tiniest of yellow flowers. She reached down and gathered some and placed them on the grave. Then she turned and walked away, but after a moment paused to glance back. The tombstone blurred before her eyes, and she cried out with horror and alarm; for it was her own name she saw inscribed upon it!

She was running again, making her way around the graves and knowing that what she had seen could be nothing more than a—a—. Oh, God, another premonition?

When she got to the stone wall she stopped breathlessly and gripped the wall until she felt some calm return. Then as though dazed, she wandered away.

It was growing late. Vickie was aware of the lengthening shadows and the setting sun. There was the West, she told herself as she veered her aimless course in that direction, but looking down she could no longer find the trail. Where had it gone? Oh, Vickie, you fool, she thought. Where have you gone? How could you have ever hoped to find Phil out here—anywhere in this place? And somewhere in her mind appeared Norman's words as though they had been written for her to memorize.

"I think you are a young woman in great danger of losing her life." And she had asked if he meant the possibility of her becoming lost while trying to find Phil. How unlikely this had seemed at the time! Then she tried to recall what his answer had been. Oh, yes. Now she remembered. He had said, "In a way." She did not know what he had meant and had dismissed the words. Now, however, she wondered if he had meant that she might lose her sanity. Here was a thought she must erase. She must not let such ideas enter her mind.

Vickie did not know what triggered the sudden knowledge that she was being followed. It was a strong sensation that felt like icy fingers on the back of her neck, and caused her to spin around and look behind her. She saw no one. But her heart pounded and she caught her breath. Her eyes peered into the gathering gloom, and something very near panic surged through her. Night falls quickly on the desert, she perceived, and the trees, the cactus, the rocks—all that had shielded her before were now becoming darkened masses that could hide someone else.

She turned and hurried on, but did not miss hearing the sound of a stone that had, apparently, been dislodged and made a rasping noise as it tumbled down a rocky ledge behind her. Oh, God! It's true. Someone is here with me.

Slowing her pace, she looked back and saw—surely it had not been imagined—a shadowy movement, and she called out, "Phil?"

Now she wondered why she had called his name. He would not be furtively following her. Then again she thought of Norman and the doubts he had about her husband. He felt that Phil was very much alive. But he might have only told her this to attempt to allay her fears that he lay dead somewhere.

She turned and hurried on, driving from her mind the incredible thoughts that had been born there. She would not look back. If the Joshuas hid her pursuer, they would also hide herself. But after a moment there was another sound and still another. Now she ran. As her feet carried her over this rough terrain, her mind moved over a worse one. It could be an animal, a coyote, or it could be a stranger waiting to attack her.

After a while she proceeded more slowly. She was exhausted and an attitude of futility was overtaking her. She could fight no longer. It was all too much. If she had been meant to die here, if it had been fate, or a diabolical plan conceived by Phil, or Norman, or Jim, then that was the way it would be. She sat down upon a rock and looked around at the darkness with an expression of hopelessness in her eyes.

She did not know how long she sat there and it did not seem to matter. Then after a time there seemed to be a glow breaking through the dark blue evening, a glow that came from two spears of light that wavered and bounced along in unison and grew nearer and nearer. And then she saw a wide ray that swung across the desert causing the trees to become tall monsters with arms raised in protest at this intrusion.

She sat immobile and watched as the lights approached, and now she heard the car's engine growing louder and louder. Then the light found her, this blinding beam turned her way, the car came to a halt and someone emerged.

"Mrs. Bishop?"

She looked at the uniformed figure and nodded.

"Everyone's been very worried about you. Don't you know you should never—"

"Yes, I know," she replied, rising to her feet. "I was only trying to find my husband, and I—I became lost."

As the patrol car drove through the gates of the Flor de Desierto, Vickie saw the front door of the house swing open and Norman's body silhouetted in the light from the hall. He appeared very tall, very stern, and she felt quite like a small child who had run away and was being brought home to face an irate parent.

"Thank God, Vickie, that you've been found. Where were you? Where did you go?"

The patrol car left, and then she answered him. "I went for a walk, that's all."

"You went for a walk! Vickie!"

"I don't care to discuss it," she said, as she walked ahead of him into the hallway. "I'm not a child who must answer to you or anyone else regarding my actions."

"I see. And it doesn't matter to you that you've caused us no end of concern, and that two patrol cars were out looking for you?"

"I am sorry about that. I really am. I had no idea that I'd become lost."

"Well, come have some dinner."

"I don't feel like eating anything."

"You need food. Come on," he said in a brusque voice. Then in a softer tone asked her if she'd like a drink and she nodded.

A martini had never tasted better, and with it in her hand she walked with him to the kitchen. "Where's Jim?" she asked.

"He's gone to Palm Springs to see if Phil arrived."

"Oh. Oh, dear! You wanted to go with him, didn't you?"

"Yes, I did. If your husband does appear, I might have been able to learn some things I've been curious about."

"But you couldn't leave because of me. Norman, I am sorry."

"I don't understand why you did it," he said.

"No, I don't suppose you do." She sat at the table and watched as he heated something on the stove. Then as a coffeepot began to send forth its tantalizing aroma she decided that she was hungry after all.

"Norman—there's somebody out there." He looked at her questioningly. "There's someone out on the desert."

"Who?"

"How would I know?"

"Okay. Describe him to me."

"I didn't actually see a person, only a shadow that moved. But I was followed. This I know. I could hear—things."

"Vickie there are many desert creatures that come out at night."

"I suppose so, but . . . " She shook her head.

"They scramble over the rocks and scurry everywhere. At night it's possible to hear all sorts of puzzling sounds, if you're listening for them."

"I found them to be more terrifying than puzzling," she admitted. And she thought of the voice calling to her, and the cemetery. "Norman, I—I came across your sister's grave."

He stared at her in surprise. "How did you get back in there?"

"I walked."

"Of course, I meant . . . It's quite an old place, isn't it?"

"Very." she said.

"I can see you are wondering why she was buried there."

"It's none of my business."

"Vickie, it's because she wanted to be. That old cemetery was interesting to her. She even thought it— picturesque. And she loved the desert. She loved the freedom of it, the mystery, the charm, as she called it."

Vickie nodded. "I understand," she said.

"Do you, Vickie? Well, I don't. I could never understand Kathleen and some of the things she did, anymore than I can understand you, and what you did today. Frankly I don't and never have, understood women, and I long ago gave up trying to." Then he smiled at her. "Perhaps this is one of the reasons they intrigue me so much."

"But you're not married, are you?" she asked.

"No, but I have been. We were juniors in college. It was all quite romantic, but not durable." He placed a slice of ham and a mound of fried potatoes before her. Then, from the refrigerator brought out a salad. "I'm not much of a cook, Vickie, but this will keep you from starving to death."

"It looks and smells delicious. And thank you. You were right. I need food. Norman, I've never before been through a day like this one. I'm glad it's almost over."

"Amen to that."

"When do you think Jim will be back?"

He shook his head. "I don't know. He may hang around the airport for some time. I would suggest that you not stay up and wait for him."

She looked at him closely. "You really feel that Phil won't be with him, don't you?" she asked.

"Vickie—I don't really know." He reached across the table and gripped her hand. "Today while driving along the roads looking for you, I gave your disappearing act quite a lot of thought, and wasn't at all pleased with the conclusion I reached. I had thought you believed me, but then I knew that you didn't." He smiled at her. "It is written that a man convinced against his will, is of the same opinion still."

She lowered her eyes from his, and felt his hand squeeze hers before he released it. "And, Vickie," he added, "this is doubly true of a woman."

"Norman, I think I will go to bed now. I'm very tired."

"That's not surprising. I'll see you in the morning. I'm going to wait up for Helen. She's being driven here by a friend of her brother-in-law."

At the door she turned and looked back at him uncertainly. I want you to like me, she longed to say. I want you to understand. "Good night, Norman."

"Good night, Vickie. I'm sure tomorrow will be a better day. Things have a way of working themselves out, you know."

But do they? She wondered this as she climbed the stairs to the balcony. Yes. Yes, of course they work themselves out—for the better—or the worse. Which was it to be?

She sighed with weariness, depression and fear. Fear had become like a heavy cape hanging from her shoulders. It weighted her down; and she could not free herself from it, for it was fastened at her throat with strong cords woven of distrust, bewilderment, hopelessness and tragedy. And the knot had been tied by the fingers of fate, and pulled taut with a seething hatred that lived within this house.

As she closed her door behind her and bolted it, she wondered what tomorrow was to bring. Overwhelmed by exhaustion, she sank rapidly into sleep.

9

WHEN VICKIE WAKENED she thought it was noon, because the light coming through the draperies was so brilliant and golden. Then she remembered she was not in San Francisco. She sighed, turned over and closed her eyes again, but sleep would not return. With a feeling of resignation, she got up.

She crossed the room and opened the closet door, then reached out hesitantly to touch Phil's suit. Just the feel of it seemed to bring him close to her, and she ran her fingers along the lapel and then down one sleeve. In the bathroom she touched his robe, left on the hook in back of the bathroom door. In the medicine cabinet she found and opened his after-shave and inhaled its fragrance.

Looking at her own possessions she came to a decision. This would be her last day here. She would stay this one more day, and then, if Phil did not call or come back, she would leave. Tomorrow morning Jim or Norman could drive her to the airport and she would go home.

She showered and dressed and arriving downstairs heard voices in the kitchen. It was here she found Helen and Norman. "I don't believe you two have met," Norman said.

"Mrs. Pomares was kind enough to inquire if we needed anything the night Phil and I arrived," Vickie said, as she extended her hand toward this woman whose gray-blue eyes bore evidence of tears.

"Mrs. Bishop," Helen murmured. And Vickie found that the hand in hers was trembling. She also noticed that Mrs. Pomares was one of those attractive ageless kind of women, with wavy dark hair and a tall, slender figure. Her face, as Vickie had noticed when she first saw her, resembled her daughter's. It even wore that same expression of distrust and fear that had been Anita's. A thought sprung into Vickie's mind, a question: Did Helen fear Jim—or was it Kathleen's ghost that frightened her?

"May I help prepare breakfast?" Vickie asked. "I—I really would like to assist in some way. I know that—that you . . . "

"I think we have everything under way," Norman said. "How do you feel this morning, Vickie?"

"Better, thank you."

"Would you like coffee?" Helen asked.

"Yes, but let me pour it."

Breakfast was a quiet meal, and a curtain of gloom seemed to have moved into the room to enclose them; it was a smothering kind of atmosphere that made it difficult for Vickie to swallow. She noticed that Helen, too, ate little, but that Norman, apparently unaware of the somberness seemed relaxed and pensive. Couldn't he see, Vickie wondered, how pale and taut Helen's face was becoming? Didn't he sense how she appeared to be gathering all the strength she could, to keep her emotions under control? Vickie hoped the woman would win the battle waging within her, and would not suddenly burst into tears or become hysterical.

Dreading the thought of such an occurrence, Vickie searched her mind for something to say to avert it, but words would not come. Tomorrow, she thought. Tomorrow I will be leaving all this, and the time cannot come too soon.

"If there is nothing here that I can do to help, I would like to go home tomorrow morning," she heard herself say. "Uh—Norman, would you be able to drive me to the airport?"

"Oh, but Vickie . . . " he said, looking at her with a mixture of surprise and incredulity in his eyes and voice. He had put down his fork and lifting his coffee cup he sipped at it and studied her over its rim.

She glanced toward Helen, who also watched her, and she wondered if she had said the wrong thing, that she was being heartless wanting to leave so soon after what had happened. They knew, now, that she was timid and wanted to run away. Her cheeks flushed. She had not meant to be selfish or weak. It was only . . .

Norman's eyes appeared pensive. "Vickie, must you go so soon?"

"I feel I might as well, however . . . "

"I think it will be Wednesday," Helen said thoughtfully.

Vickie looked at her.

"The funeral," Norman murmured.

"Oh—Oh, yes. I want to send flowers. Let me know where . . . " Vickie replied softly.

"I never should have left her," Helen cried out. "Knowing Anita was so distressed, I should not have gone away. I am to blame. I should have known."

"Don't blame yourself," Norman said firmly. "If it was anyone's fault, it was ours, Jim's and mine. We thought she had run off into the desert. Never once did we think of the . . . " He could not seem to go on.

Vickie looked from one of them to the other. Because Kathleen had been found out there in the sand, it was quite natural, really, to assume that Anita surely would follow, especially since she was burdened with the horror that lived in her mind. "She calls my name," the girl had said. "She calls from the hills." Vickie recalled that this was the direction in which Jim had taken to find the missing girl.

Now Vickie shuddered as she pictured again that flowing wisp of vapor that had followed Anita from the room. Here was a scene that she would never forget, and she thought of how she had neglected to say a word, how she had feared the men would doubt her sanity. I share the guilt, she told herself. Perhaps I am at fault more than they, because surely it was the ghost of Kathleen who pushed Vickie into the well to drown. But this thought is insane, and one I must reveal to no one—ever.

Norman and Helen still talked; tentative plans were being discussed regarding the funeral, but Vickie did not listen to the words. She turned her thoughts to going home. Tomorrow, she thought. If I can just get through these grief-laden hours until tomorrow, then I will be out of this house, this flower of the desert that I entered knowing full well that I was making a mistake. A hunch? A premonition? Why didn't I listen? Why didn't I heed the warning? But I will heed it now. I will go home.

Now she felt Helen's eyes turned toward her. Oh, God, she pleaded, don't let her know that I am in any way responsible for her daughter's death. That would be more than I could bear.

It was mid-morning before Jim appeared. He must have

just entered the downstairs hall when the telephone rang,
and immediately he answered it, while Vickie, in the kitch-
en with Helen, held her breath. Then after a moment she
turned toward the silent woman. "I—I thought it might be
my husband," she explained, as her hand fluttered nervously to her throat. "He—he seems to be missing."

"Missing? Your husband?" Helen asked incredulously.

"Well—his car has been found abandoned. Of course, it's
quite possible that it was stolen from the airport and then
left not far off the road, behind some rocks, half hidden
from view. Isn't it strange though that the car had been
driven so near this house? I don't think it's more than two or
three miles away."

Helen looked at her and nodded. "It is strange," she
replied. "But, it could have happened that someone did
steal it. It's certainly not uncommon. Did your husband fly
somewhere? I mean, you said the car was left at the airport."

"Yes. You know when he and Jim left here to go to Palm
Springs? Well, while there Phil learned he had to return to
San Francisco to have some papers signed. In fact, he
called me from the airport to tell me."

"Then you mustn't worry. He is in San Francisco."

"But I haven't been able to reach him there, and he told
me he would try to get back here last night, but—he
didn't."

Vickie saw the sadness in Helen's eyes, and she said,
"Oh, forgive me! How selfish I am to pour out my troubles
to you at a time like this! They're nothing compared to
yours. I am sorry."

"Everyone has troubles and grief that they must bear,"
the woman said softly.

"I think you are very brave," Vickie told her sincerely.
"You have the kind of strength I admire and wish I possessed."

"It comes with time," Helen said. "Death took my husband from me too. After awhile we learn to stop thrashing out at Fate. We learn to accept, and to go on."

Vickie understood Norman's feelings about Helen. She was an extraordinary person.

"Helen." The voice was Jim's.

They turned to see him entering the room. Immediately he walked toward her and tenderly, which was his way, placed his arm around the woman's shoulders. Norman had been right, Vickie decided. Helen was not particularly fond of her employer, because she pulled away rather quickly, and the moment became one of embarrassment.

"Would you like some coffee?" Vickie asked him. He looked at her and nodded. "Thanks. I would."

"I'll scramble you a couple of eggs, also."

He sat at the table and Vickie in a low voice spoke to Helen. "Why don't you go to your room? I know there must be things you want to do." Then after she was gone, Jim shook his head and looked gratefully toward Vickie.

"It's rough," he said, "what she's going through. I don't know how to help her."

"There's little we can do," she told him. "Jim, have you heard anything about Phil?"

"Nothing. The search will be accelerated today. A helicopter will be used, this morning, I think." And a faraway look came into his eyes. He was remembering, remembering the time six months ago when . . .

"Vickie, where did you go yesterday?"

"Where could I go, but out there—and look for him?"

He nodded. "I understand. It was something you felt you had to do. You would never have been happy if you hadn't tried to find him yourself."

"That's right."

"Do you feel now that he isn't out there?"

"I don't know. All I learned was how futile it is to search for even a trace of a person who might have wandered off into such a place as this desert."

"I know," he said and his eyes darkened.

And now as she put a plate of food before him she looked with doubt at this man who had been the one to find his wife in the vastness of this wasteland. He alone had found her. The feat seemed impossible, and a nagging suspicion returned to haunt her. Was Norman correct? Was it really Jim who had been the cause of Kathleen's death?

"Where is Norman?" he asked.

"I—I don't know. He built a fire in the living room after breakfast, and then . . . " She shrugged. "Perhaps he's in his room."

"There are some things he and I must take care of. First, your husband's car is to be towed away today. It will be held until you or he decide what should be done with it. The motor is filled with sand, and—"

"Phil or I? You do feel that he is alive, don't you?" she asked.

"Vickie, I've told you he flew to San Francisco, but you haven't been able to believe me."

"I don't think you lied, Jim. Why should you? But I feel that he came back, picked up his car and drove it—to where it is. Quite likely he ran out of gas. The puzzling part is that the car is several yards off the road and in between those rocks. I can't understand why, unless it was because he was blinded by the storm and couldn't see where he was going."

His eyes avoided hers. She noticed this. "I don't know," he said. "I just don't know." Then with his eyes still on his plate he continued. "After Norman and I see about the car, then there are certain—formalities to be taken care of

with the authorities regarding Anita's death, since it was—
what it was. The telephone call I just received concerned
this matter."

"Oh. Oh, of course."

"Unfortunately, they wanted to ask Helen some questions about Anita, hoping to uncover a clue as to her
reason for taking her own life. I was able to persuade them
to postpone this ordeal for a few days. After all, it's too
soon to put her through an interrogation. She's had
enough."

Vickie nodded. "I think she said the funeral is to be
Wednesday."

"Oh?"

"I don't know where it will be."

"I'll help her take care of everything," he said.

"Jim, unless there is some need for my being here, I
want to go home tomorrow."

Now his eyes raised to hers. "I—I wish you wouldn't," he
said hesitantly. "Vickie, please stay a little longer. I want
you to; I want you to, very, very much."

"But, I—"

"Vickie, if you leave, then I'll be alone here; more alone
than I have ever been before." She saw a pleading in his
eyes. "Vickie, I'm not a bad guy. All I ask is that you give
me a chance to prove a few things to you. Damn it! I could
make you happy, if you'd let me."

"You're forgetting something, aren't you?"

"What?"

"I have a husband—haven't I?"

His eyes left hers now. He took a deep breath and
inhaled slowly. "Phil is not worth your little finger," he
said. At that point Norman entered the room.

Vickie decided to use this opportunity to escape this
embarrassing situation. "Perhaps I can be of some help to
Helen. Excuse me."

As she walked through the dining room she wondered

how much of the conversation had been overheard by Norman. The expression on his face indicated something— was it anger?

In the hall she glanced toward the living room and saw that the draperies had not as yet been opened. She approached the doorway and felt a kind of damp penetrating cold that hovered there. A small fire had been built. It crackled and hissed on the hearth, and seemed to be struggling uselessly to heat the enormous room. It would soon give up and dwindle to ashes, she knew, and she hurried now away from this room and along the hall to where a door opened onto the patio.

The brilliance of the sky was almost startling. This was a sapphire day, and the warmest one since she had arrived here. It was going to be like the day when she and Anita had walked across the sand and the light had been so dazzling that Vickie had been conscious of tiny specks floating before her eyes.

Hesitantly she approached the two rooms to her left. The door was open to Anita's room, and the one next to it, Helen's, was closed. "Mrs. Pomares?" she called.

"Yes?" came the reply from Anita's room.

"I—I was wondering if there was something I could do to help you," Vickie said.

Then Helen appeared. She had been crying again, and now dabbed at her eyes with a tissue. "Thank you, Mrs. Bishop. As a matter of fact I could use another pair of hands. I want to pack my daughter's belongings as well as my own. I don't intend to stay here, of course." She nodded toward the well. "I could never live in this place again."

"I understand. Just tell me what I can do."

"Well—" With a trembling hand she indicated a suitcase open on the bed. "I have been trying to bring myself to pack Anita's clothing, but—it is so difficult."

"I'll do it, Mrs. Pomares. You pack your own things."

A small sigh of relief escaped from the woman's lips. "Thank you. You're very kind. And call me Helen. Please?'

"Of course." Vickie saw the opened dresser drawers. "I suppose you want to take everything, Helen?"

"Yes. Yes, I think so, at least for now. Someday I will be able to sort out what was hers and dispose of what I do not want to keep. As you can see she didn't have much, and neither do I. Most young girls want so much, but Anita didn't seem to care. She was a rather—odd girl, not like others her age. When I was twenty I wanted all the clothes I could get, and I liked being around people, many people. How I loved to dance and laugh and enjoy myself! I was happy then. When I was twenty I was happy."

On the top of Anita's dresser stood a small heart-shaped jewelry box, and her mother opened it. "Look," she said; "only two Mexican silver bracelets, three strands of beads, and a pair of earrings. She very seldom wore these. Always she had on her ears tiny gold loops, and around her neck a thin chain with a cross. They aren't here, so she must have been wearing them when—yesterday when . . . "

"Yes," Vickie murmured. "Yes, I think she was."

"And her clothes," Helen continued, "She liked those of Mexico. She never should have been brought here. I was wrong to take her away."

"She wasn't unhappy," Vickie said, and knew she spoke only a half-truth. "Did you like living in Mexico?"

"At first I did. It was all so different and exciting, like going on a trip, a vacation, but then, after a while . . . Life for a woman is different there, Mrs. Bishop. I missed the freedom that I was used to, but . . . " She shrugged. "I gave up struggling against my lot. I lived as the other senoras did and the years passed. After Juan, my husband died, I spent many months thinking. I was so frightened, there was so little money, and I didn't know what on earth to do. It took so much courage to come back here, but I could not stay there, either. There were days when I thought I would go mad, trying to decide what I should do. Now, since what happened, I know I must have made the wrong decision."

"No," Vickie told her. "You did what was right."

"But Anita and I were terrified trying to work and make a place for ourselves in this country after so many years of living such a quiet life. If it had not been for Norman, Mr. Corbett, I don't know what we would have done."

Vickie looked at herself in the dresser mirror. Norman had told the truth about Helen and Anita, she realized, and longed to question the woman about some other things, but this was hardly the time. Helen went to the next room and Vickie began to pack the dead girl's clothing, thinking that her mother had been right. Anita should have remained in Mexico. It was where she was meant to live. Only death had waited for the unfortunate girl here, here at the Flor de Desierto. Death had waited here for Kathleen, also, Vickie thought with a quick shudder. And Phil, had it waited here for Phil?

And then another unanswered question crept into her mind. Who else, she wondered? Who else was to become its victim? In the mirror she caught an unexpected reflection of herself, and behind her, through the window of the room, was mirrored the well. She gasped and spun around, shaken by the thoughts that hounded her. One thing she knew. She must leave. She must leave this house and what was here before it was too late. If Phil came back tonight, or if he did not, she would leave tomorrow morning.

10

Feverishly Vickie packed Anita's clothing. Norman appeared at the door, and speaking to both Helen and her, he explained that there were certain matters to be taken care of, and that he and Jim would be gone most of the day. "In fact," he said, his eyes on Vickie's, "if we are detained too long at Yucca Valley, then we'll go on from there to Palm Springs, so don't be surprised if we aren't back in time for dinner. The airport, Vickie," he said. "Jim and I feel we should go there once again—just in case."

She nodded gratefully. "Thank you," she replied, and then, seeing that Helen had left her door and vanished into the closet that was hers, she whispered to him. "They won't want to question me, will they? I hope not."

"I don't know, Vickie, but I hardly think so. Don't worry about it."

"Norman, Helen wants to leave as soon as possible, so don't you think it would be all right if I left here tomorrow? There is nothing I can do to help her, not really. Actually, she might want to go tomorrow also." Her eyes went to the well. "And who can blame her?" she added.

"I can't keep you here against your will, Vickie." The way his eyes looked into hers—searchingly, made her heart beat faster.

"Norman, it's just that I . . . You understand, don't you?"

He nodded and then in a hushed voice said, "Vickie, I have the feeling that this is my last day here, also. I, too, may be leaving tomorrow. The time has come to place my cards on the table, to have a showdown with Jim, and tonight will give me this opportunity."

"Tonight? You mean if Phil doesn't come back?"

"If he doesn't, I'm going to find out why, and then I think I'll learn why Kathleen died, for somehow there must be a connecting thread."

"Jim will tell you nothing."

"He'll tell me if I have to . . . "

"Oh, Norman!"

"Don't forget, Vickie, I have information about him. Wait until I reveal what I know! Jim Burant is going to be quite surprised." He squeezed her hand. "I'll see you later." He walked away then, across the patio, and at the well he paused and looked back at her.

"Norman," she said, hurrying after him. "Be careful. Please be careful."

His eyebrows raised with surprise. "I think you mean that," he said.

She caught her breath. "I—I think I do," she whispered.

He smiled and then walked toward the garage. After a moment she heard a car back out and drive away. He and Jim had gone together, of course, and she wondered which car they had taken. Who would be at the wheel? And now a chilling sense of impending disaster came over her. Who would be coming back?

She returned to Anita's room and finished the packing with a kind of frantic urgency. Then she joined Helen who stood amid a confusing variety of belongings. "Would you help me?" she asked. "I want to get my things together, so I can leave tomorrow. My brother-in-law will be coming here to pick me up and I must be ready." She sighed. "I should discard so much that is here, and yet . . . " She shook her head. "Everything I touch brings a kind of aching memory. You know I've lived here a year—Anita and I—a long year, and . . . "

"Why don't we have a sandwich and some tea," Vickie suggested, and then we'll feel more like doing this. Shall we?"

"Yes. Yes, that is a good idea. You know, Mrs. Bishop, after what's happened it makes it difficult for me to get my thoughts organized as well as my meager possessions."

A year, Vickie was thinking, as they crossed the patio and entered the hallway. If Norman has told me the truth about Phil's being here before, then Helen would be the one to verify this. But then, what would Helen think? She would wonder why I didn't know of his former visit or visits. And then, too, Vickie reminded herself, this was not the time to ask such a question. Only yesterday this woman had lost her daughter. Only yesterday? Vickie felt that it had been almost a lifetime since then.

During lunch Helen talked of Mexico City, her marriage, her life. It was as though she wanted to relive every moment of it. And she talked of Anita. Anita as a baby, a small child, a very young girl beginning to bloom, and the last years of her life. Vickie listened closely keeping her mind on Helen's words for in this way she could not dwell on the frightening possibilities that nagged and worried her, these doubts that darted in and out of her thoughts.

It might have been the food, or it could have been the words Helen had spoken, relieving her mind of pent-up memories, but once they returned to the room she had occupied, they were able to accomplish their mission. Three suitcases were packed, and the articles Helen no longer wanted, they placed in a carton from the laundry.

"Why don't you rest now?" Vickie said. "You do look tired. Was it late when you arrived last night?"

"Nearly midnight," she said with a nod. "I think I would like to lie down for a while."

After Vickie closed the door behind her she went to her own room, pulled the bag out of the closet and began to pack. She placed Phil's suit into it first, then his shoes and two shirts and some underwear that he had placed in a drawer. Like Helen, every article Vickie touched brought a kind of aching memory. Now she added what was hers; everything except her nightgown and the suit that she would wear tomorrow. Tomorrow. Would it ever come?

She crossed to the window and looked at the view. Here was a scene she would never see again. Tomorrow afternoon she would be looking at the bay instead of the desert. Tomorrow she would be in her own apartment, and pensively she thought of Phil's clothes that would be there, and his magazines, his golf clubs. Everywhere she would turn she would see him and what was his. Like Helen, she should weep, but tears would not come. There were too many doubts, too many unanswered questions.

Then in her mind she saw, as though it stood out there in the midst of the desert where her eyes were wandering, a tombstone, a fence around the mound, a cemetery from so long ago, and she felt very close to Kathleen. Surely she is not there, she is here, she told herself. She is close to me, for she understands. She, too, knew love and jealousy and loneliness. She, too, had been betrayed. She, too, had married the wrong man.

That evening Vickie and Helen sat at the large table in the kitchen and ate a simple dinner. It was after seven and the desert had already become lavender and blue with long shadows and the promise of a star-studded sky. "Have you liked living here?" Vickie asked. "It's a beautiful house."

"Beautiful, yes," said the woman, "but everyone who enters it is doomed."

Vickie's eyes narrowed. "Why do you say that?" she asked.

"After what has happened, how can I feel any other way?" she replied. "First it ruined my daughter's life and then it killed her."

Vickie nodded. "Like—Mrs. Burant. Kathleen."

"Mrs. Burant hated Anita," Helen said.

"Oh, surely not," Vickie replied quickly. "Your daughter was such a dear person."

"And Mrs. Burant was very jealous. She was so jealous of Anita, it frightened me at times. You did not know her, did you?"

"No."

"She looked very much like you, and could be sweet and kind just like you, but—she had a temper like something out of hell. You have no idea."

"Oh, really? Did—did Mr. Burant find it difficult to live happily with his wife?" Vickie was shocked at her own effrontery.

The gray-blue eyes widened. "Oh, you have no idea! He began to drink too much, and I became so nervous because of all the turmoil here, that my doctor prescribed tranquilizers for me. It seems strange that with all the sunshine outside this house, nothing but evil and gloominess lived within—bringing the madness. I'll tell you a secret. My Anita had it, this insanity, and looking back I now know Mrs. Burant must have had it, too. That's why she died as she did, wandering off all alone out there. Now I think it was the reason for her behavior, her jealousy and her temper. These were born in her sick mind."

"Perhaps," Vickie said uncertainly.

"It had to be that," the woman insisted. "Mrs. Burant was very familiar with this area, so how else could she have become lost?"

"I—don't believe it would be very difficult," Vickie said.

"I would feel sorry about what happened to her except for one thing," Helen continued, while she dabbed at new tears that had sprung into her eyes. "Even though she was not responsible for her actions, I know if it had not been for her, my daughter would be alive today. This is something I cannot forget or forgive. For this I hate the house and everyone in it. This is a house of death. Mrs. Bishop, do you know that a man lost his life here while the well was being dug?"

"No, I hadn't heard about that."

"He fell into it and a drill went right through him. That marks a house, or anything being constructed. It's as though death and tragedy have been built into the place; becoming a part of it, like the wood and bricks and concrete. And nothing can change its fate. It is destined to bring despair to all who come within its walls."

"Oh, but . . . " Vickie sat quite still holding a cup in her hand halfway between the saucer and her lips. How dare she deny the truth of what this woman was saying, when the evidence was all around them? Who was happy here? Kathleen had not been, and had died. Anita had not been, and she too, was dead. Norman? Jim? Helen? Herself? All troubled. We still live, she told herself, but for how long? And Phil!

"Helen!" Vickie said suddenly, "I don't know if my husband is dead or alive," and the cup slipped from her hand, hit the edge of the table and shattered against the tile floor. "Oh, dear. Look what I've done."

Helen rose from the table as Vickie did. "I'll clean it up, Helen," she said. "How clumsy that was of me!"

"No, I'll do it," the woman said as she went to the laundry and service area and returned with a broom and dust pan. "You do believe, just as I do that this house is cursed."

Vickie looked at Helen thoughtfully. How can I say, she wondered, that this woman is only superstitious, after what I have seen here? The figure outside my door. The mist following Anita from the room before she was drowned. The icy chill. The laughter in the wind. The fingers tapping against the window pane. The presence of the unseen. And yesterday—the voice that called my name. Can I say that this poor, grieved woman is wrong? Can I tell her I don't believe in what I can't understand—when I do? When I feel this terror that is around me, like a rattlesnake about to strike?

"I don't know if the house is cursed. Perhaps it is. I don't believe we entirely realize the strange and powerful forces that fashion our lives," she replied. "I don't believe we should blame ourselves for the cards that have been dealt us." Now she frowned with bewilderment. These words she had just spoken, could they be hers? Vickie could not recall ever uttering such an opinion before. Secretly she believed in premonitions, but these were warnings, giving one a chance to avoid a possible disaster, she had felt. Always she had believed that each person was responsible for his own actions. Master of his fate. Captain of his soul. Was her philosophy changing? If not, then why was she speaking lines foreign to her? It was as though she were playing the role of someone else.

She looked at Helen thoughtfully, as the woman poured the tiny bits of china into the wastebasket. It was all Vickie could do to refrain from asking when Phil had been here before, and had Helen, perhaps, learned the reason for his visit. Had she overheard words being spoken between Jim and Phil? But then, Norman had seen such fear on Helen's face when she had let this bit of information slip from her lips. She would not want to speak of it now. Then, Vickie, gazing at the back of the woman's head, wondered something else. If she knew that Jim was responsible for his wife's death, why did she shield him and remain here, she and Anita?

"You are quite right," she heard Helen say. "We should not blame ourselves. I can say that I am to blame for Anita's death, because I brought her here, or because I left her for a short time, even though I knew she wasn't well. And Norman can say the fault was his and Jim's. And you, Mrs. Bishop; somewhere in your mind may be a feeling of guilt about her death. But what fools we are to torture ourselves this way. Actually, I should not even blame Kathleen. Anita only followed the course that was to be hers, just as we all do. I cannot forgive Jim's wife, as I have told you, but this is the way I was meant to feel. We think alike, Mrs. Bishop."

Vickie nodded uncertainly and began to help Helen remove the dishes from the table. "You are a guest, Mrs. Bishop," the woman said, "and should not be helping me with my work, but I do appreciate it. Yesterday and today have been terrible for me, and I can't see what the future has in store, but then who can? All I know now, is that I am very tired—so tired."

"Then please let me finish these alone," Vickie told her. "Really I don't mind, and I need something to do while waiting for Jim and Norman and . . . "

"And your husband," Helen said. "I hope he is with them."

"Thank you. Now, why don't you go to bed and try to get some rest?"

"You wouldn't mind?"

"I insist," Vickie said.

After Helen had gone, Vickie worked quickly, and after the last dish was put away, she stood in the kitchen and looked around her. This is the last night, she told herself. Never again will I stand inside this house after darkness. Never will I be conscious of the silence around me, the feeling of being alone in the middle of a vast sea of sand and strange, grotesque vegetation. Alone? She glanced toward the door leading to the dining room. Were she and Helen really alone in the house?

Forcibly she shook this feeling from her. She must control her imagination, she told herself. But the dining room seemed so dark, so . . . But wait. She didn't need to enter it to get to the balcony. There was a door to the patio leading from the garage. She could go through the service area, the storage room, and into the garage. From there she could enter the hall and up the inside stairway, or she could climb the one on the outside of the house, if she wished. She felt relieved, because in this way she could not only avoid the dining room, but the living room as well. There was no need to go near them.

She found the service area dreary, and crossed it quickly to the door leading into the storage room. She opened it and found the switch that turned on a single light, a bare bulb hanging from the ceiling that revealed a shadowy scene of quiet interest. The things people keep, she thought. A broken bar stool, several lamps, unbelievably dusty golf clubs, bric-a-brac. There were suitcases, trunks and many boxes; they, too, laden with dust. Lonely items, discarded and forgotten, bringing to her a feeling of gloom.

On her way to the garage she followed a path through the room's contents, and then paused with a hesitant expression on her face, as if a hand had reached out to detain her. It would take but a moment, she thought, to open a box, or lift the lid of an unlocked trunk.

Stacked upon the nearest large carton were old magazines, gray with a dusty veil, and as she lifted them she recoiled as something scurried away to hide, something perhaps two inches long, a colorless creature with a segmented tail. A scorpion. She waited motionless until she was assured that the venomous little terror had been as frightened from their encounter as she was, then cautiously lifted the lid to the cardboard box.

Books. Here were countless volumes, thick and thin, large and small, and with an uncanny sensation that a hand drew her own into the box, she withdrew a scrapbook, and opened it. It was filled with snapshots and clippings, and soon she realized that what she held were pictures of Jim Burant and stories of sports events. So—he had played football at the University of California, six years before she herself had attended there. But wait—she had gone to Berkeley, while he attended in Los Angeles, U.C.L.A. The same as Phil! Six years ago? Yes! He and Phil had been in the same class!

Glancing quickly around the room she found a trunk, less dusty than the others, and sat upon it while her trembling hands flipped the pages before her until she found what she knew must be here. Then with a cold numbness she read a list of names. Philip Bishop, James Burant— fraternity brothers.

Her legs and arms felt leaden as she returned the book to its place in the box and closed the lid. One by one Norman's words were proving to be correct. What she had not wanted to believe was true. Fear seemed to wrap itself around her. What did it all mean? What had taken place? And now what was meant to happen?

The objects in the room seemed to swim and blur before her eyes, then gradually she saw the trunk where she had been sitting, and observed it thoughtfully. It seemed to be the only container in the room that had been opened within the last few years. She stared at it. The lid was not covered with dust! Then it had been opened—recently! She gasped, and the thought that exploded in her mind made her cry out with horror. "Phil!"

"No! No!" she heard herself murmur as she approached it slowly as one wading through water. It couldn't be. He was missing, but—it just couldn't be.

A powerful feeling of dread, like nothing she had ever known before almost immobilized her. Could she open this trunk? And if—if . . . Oh, God! Would she be able to endure the sight of what might be inside?

Now she tried to back away, while all the time knowing that she must see what was concealed here. Whatever had, with fear, made her avoid the dining room and had led her into this room of the past; whatever had directed her hand to the book and the list of names, would not let her leave now. Taking a deep breath, she reached down and found the trunk was not locked. With her eyes closed, she lifted the lid. She waited a moment for strength to come to her, and then opened her eyes.

A sigh of deep relief burst from her lips, and she brushed away the mist of perspiration that covered her brow. Here, in careless disorder, lay a jumble of women's clothing. The entire trunk was filled with garments that must have belonged to Kathleen. Vickie, looking at the colorful array, shook as she tried to control the hysterics that had been waiting for two days to erupt. Hesitantly she touched a red velvet formal, and saw a spot suddenly

appear where a tear from her eyes dropped on the materi-
al. She lifted the dress from the trunk and attempted to
rub away the mark, then with a sob, realized that it no
longer mattered. Kathleen would never wear the dress
again.

Looking back into the trunk, its contents blurred as she
brushed away the tears. Vickie stared, mystified, not being
sure that what she saw was really there. Pale blue, silvery
blue chiffon. Her fingers trembled as she lifted it, this long
and flowing peignor, and immediately she dropped it
again, choking back a scream that was in her throat. The
blue and gray shadow beside the wall! The billowing garment on the figure outside her door!

Had she cried aloud? Vickie was not sure. She contemplated this heap of sheer fabric as it had fallen, and it was
then she saw what had been lying beneath it. One tendril
coiled out, and hesitantly she reached down and moved
aside the robe to find a cascade of shimmering gold. A
wig. One that must have been very much like Kathleen's
own hair. Thoughtfully she ran her hand along her cheek
until a wisp of her own titian hair was entangled in her
fingers. Blonde like mine, she was thinking, but less red.

Her throat turned dry and she gasped with the possibility that was presenting itself. If someone wore this wig and
this peignor—if someone stood by the well at night, or
outside her door on the balcony, or—

"Mrs. Bishop!"

Vickie froze, then whirled around to find a face glaring
at her from the doorway. There was an icy hatred in the
gray-blue eyes, and now a slow and insidious smile was
forming on the woman's lips.

"Helen!" Vickie gasped. "It was you!"

Suddenly all was darkness as the light was switched off.
Vickie had no chance to scream or move before her arm
was painfully grasped—and then her throat. The woman's

fingernails were digging into her flesh, and the strength of those hands stunned her. Then Vickie lashed out with her free arm, striking Helen's face, and she heard the hissed oaths that escaped the woman's lips. She tried to loosen the grip around her throat, fighting like a tigress, clawing frantically until she felt her lungs would burst. Then suddenly she seemed to be lost in clouds of chiffon and the faint scent of floral perfume closed around her as the world turned to a velvet blackness.

With a shocking horror she felt the solid sides and top of this—this tomb that confined her. In a wild panic she thrashed and pounded with her fists. The trunk! Oh, no! God, no! She was inside the trunk! She screamed again and again, while the sound of her voice seemed to press in around her, piercing her ears and filling her very soul.

"God Almighty, Helen!" she shrieked. "Let me out of here!"

And then she heard a laugh. There was something familiar about it. She had heard this laugh before. Where? When? And then she knew. It had been in the wind. The wind had laughed like this, hadn't it?

"Helen!" She screamed again, and with all her strength pushed against the lid of the trunk. Was it locked? She had seen no key. But Helen—Helen must have one, for this was where she had hidden Kathleen's robe and the wig. The wig—Vickie could feel the ringlets of it curling around her fingers the way she so often twisted her own hair, and a freezing shudder filled her entire being.

"Helen, please!"

There was no response.

"Helen speak to me."

"You are a fool!" The woman cried out angrily, and Vickie wept with relief. If somehow she could keep Helen here, perhaps she could persuade her to open the trunk; perhaps with someone there with whom she could talk she would not go mad in this blackness, this tightness. No! She must not think—must not let her mind dwell on the hideous fact that she was being buried alive.

She must play a different part, she told herself. That was all she could do. It was night, a dark night, and she was in her car. But she was not alone. There was a person right here beside her; a woman named Helen. But the car lights had gone out, and this was the reason it was so dark, this and the fact that there was no moon tonight.

"It's so dark, Helen," she heard herself say in a loud voice, and Helen responded again with a laugh.

Vickie fingered the wig. It was not one belonging to Kathleen, she told herself. It was Helen's and she wore it to portray her role, that of a ghost. She must have wanted to frighten her daughter into leaving this house—and Jim. Why had she gone to such measures to drive Anita away? Did she know about their relationship? Then why didn't she leave and take Anita with her instead of driving the girl out of her mind and into the well? Now she knows what she has done. Now she knows, and how does she feel? Vickie wondered.

"Helen! Helen let me out! I must talk to you!"

"Why should I speak to a fool?" Vickie heard her say. "You are such a fool that you don't even know your husband wanted you lost in the desert." And then there was that ghastly laugh again, wild and shrill.

"Helen—how do you know?" Vickie asked incredulously. There was no answer.

"What did you say about my husband?"

"Why do you think his car is out there? Why do you think he brought you here? I'll tell you why. You were to become lost in the desert while looking for him, and you were not to be found until it was too late."

"That's not true!" Vickie cried out. Helen was insane, she told herself. How terribly mad she was! "You—must be mistaken," she said determinedly, for this was what she wanted to think.

"I am not mistaken. I know. I listened at the door while they made their plans; Jim and that husband of yours. Nothing ever happened in this house that I did not know about."

Vickie parted her lips to speak, but could not. The woman did not lie. This was what Norman had suspected, what he had feared, what he hadn't wanted to tell her.

"But Jim did not carry out his part of the agreement, and after I saw you I knew why," she heard Helen say. "You are the helpless, fragile kind of woman who seems like a kitten. But hidden inside is someone else, someone vicious and mean that he can't see."

Again Vickie recalled what she had thought was an apparition outside the bedroom door. It had been Helen who stood there, curious and calculating.

"And you—you did just as you were supposed to do," Helen continued. "You went out there looking for your husband. I saw you from my trailer, and I followed you. I saw what you did. Then I called to you. 'Vickeee— Vickeee,' I said, and you listened." Now her voice became more shrill. "Her grave! You put flowers on her grave! You fool! You crazy little fool! And I followed you and followed you. How scared you were! I wish Jim could have seen you then, seen what a coward you are. He's in love with you, because you are like Kathleen. To him you are Kathleen returned."

"Kathleen is dead. He knows that," Vickie said wondering how much longer she could breathe inside this trunk. She must try to think clearly. She must say the right words. "Helen—you are wrong. He does not love me." Jim. This woman keeps speaking of Jim. Oh! That was it! Here was the reason she had tried to drive her daughter away.

"Helen," Vickie called out. "Jim killed Kathleen, and do you know why? It was because he loves you. You are the one he wants."

Would she believe this? Vickie wondered, and she inhaled the smallest bit of air knowing she should conserve as much of it as possible. Precious air. She would pretend she was diving under water. Yes, that was it. She was diving and—

"Did he tell you that he killed his wife for me?"

Vickie's hopes surged. "Yes," she gasped. "He did. That's exactly what he told me."

"You lie!" Helen shrieked. "I killed her. I put tranquilizers in her food, then, meek as a newborn puppy, she went with me to her car, and I drove her into the hills and left her there asleep, sound asleep in the warm sun; the nice warm sunshine."

"Oh, Helen!"

"With her dead I thought he would turn to me, but instead, he . . . "

Madness, this Vickie knew, but she was also aware that Helen spoke the truth. Then she placed her hands over her face. The reason it is so dark here is because I am covering my eyes, she told herself. If I take my hands away there will be light again. This is what I must believe. I must tell myself this over and over. All I need do is to take my hands away and . . .

Now she was conscious of a sound, a vague creaking, and she listened closely. Suddenly she knew. It was the lid; the trunk was not locked. Helen must be sitting on it and had now changed her position slightly. A new hope rose within her. There would be no use pressing against the top, or even attempting to lunge at it. She had tried that. It was impossible to force her way out. But there was a chance . . . If she could find something to say—words

that would bring Helen to her feet. "Oh, God!" she murmured. "Help me! Help me before it's too late."

The smothering sensation was as if a heavy blanket had
been placed against her face. "Helen!" she called out with
a note of desperation in her voice. "I know Jim is in love
with you. I—I have proof. Yes! I have—a letter."

"Helen? Can you hear me?"

There was no response. Vickie pressed her hands against
the lid of the trunk. It would not move. Helen must still be
there. She must think. She must not give up. "Helen, Jim
wrote a letter to my husband, to Phil, and—and in it he
told him that it was you he loved, but he thought you
wanted nothing to do with him. I saw the letter. I read it."

"I don't believe you."

"It's true. It's true. I have the letter with me. I can show
it to you. I found it in Phil's desk at home, and I brought it
with me."

"You're lying again."

"No! No, I'm not. Would you like to see it?"

"I don't believe you. There is no reason you would bring
such a letter here with you. If one even exists."

Vickie felt the perspiration on her face and hands. How
hot it was in here! How deadly! No air. No air. How
horrible this woman was! Evil and calculating. Why would
I bring such a letter here? Vickie wondered, searching
madly for an answer. And then it came.

"I brought it with me because Phil tried to lead me to
believe that he didn't know Jim. I thought I had better
have it in case I needed to confront him with it. I'll get it
and show it to you."

Again there was no answer.

"Helen? You would like to see it, wouldn't you? If you
read it then you would realize how Jim feels about you,
how he wants you."

"Me? He made love to Anita," the woman said with frigid hatred. "I know. I know."

"I'll tell you a secret, Helen. He never did. He only led you to believe this to make you jealous. This, too, is in the letter. He confided in Phil because they have been close friends ever since their school days."

"Where is it, this letter?"

Vickie felt faint. It was becoming more and more difficult to think clearly. If she told this woman of a place to look and she left, then . . . Vickie shook her head. No, Helen would never give her a chance to escape. Before she left this room she would stack so much weight on the trunk that lifting the lid would still be impossible. She is shrewd and sharp and dangerous. She would return here and kill her; Vickie knew this.

"Where is the letter?" Helen demanded.

"The letter—the letter," Vicky breathed. "In my luggage," she said. "But I have it very well hidden. It's in a secret pocket. You can understand why I had to conceal it in a place where Phil couldn't—where anyone else couldn't find it. Only I know how to get to it, Helen. And you should read it."

Would this ruse work? she wondered. Helen was not moving. There was not a sound. "I will lead you to it," she called hopefully.

"I can never let you out. You know too much. You have seen too much." There was a cold finality in her voice.

"Helen, I'll never tell anyone what you told me about Kathleen. Why should I? What would I have to gain? If you will let me out, then I shall be forever indebted to you. I am, even now, for you've revealed to me the kind of man I married. I am grateful for this. We're friends, Helen; you and I. You should be pleased about what I have told you. Now you know that Jim wants you very much. And

Helen, I haven't seen a thing. The robe belonged to Kathleen, just like this red velvet gown that's with it. And the wig. I know it belonged to Kathleen. I have two of them at home that I wear sometimes."

Nothing. No sound. No voice. I—I think I'm going to lose consciousness, Vickie found herself thinking, as a kind of roaring filled her ears. "Let's go, Helen—I'll—show you. I'll—"

The lid was being lifted! Vickie gasped for air and sat up, moving slowly, cautiously so Helen would not become suspicious. She looked at the face blurred in the darkness, at those eyes!

"Show me the letter," Helen said, and together they walked from the room, through the service area and into the kitchen where there was light, blessed light.

Now they entered the dining room; once more Vickie's eyes gazed at the windows where she had heard the soft sound of fingers against the glass. Helen's? She had said that nothing happened in this house that she did not know about. She must have been out there listening, this woman who now gripped her wrist so tightly. Could she have been here all the time? Had Norman lied about taking her to Los Angeles?

They walked along the hallway and as they climbed the stairs Vickie found herself counting. Ten, eleven, twelve, thirteen—thirteen steps to the gallows. Unless she could think of a way to escape, she was indeed walking with her executioner at her side. How would Helen kill her? When no letter could be produced, how was she to die? Pushed from the balcony? The well? Was that what lay in wait for her? Helen was tall and strong. What chance had she against such a foe?

At the top of the stairs, Helen opened the door and they stepped out onto the balcony. Vickie was startled to find the night so beautiful. She was conscious of the moonlight, and the stars; surely there had never been so many before. My last night of being alive, she thought, and it is now I see the beauty of it all. The earth, the sky, the timelessness of space. I am viewing eternity.

They had reached her room, and Helen opened the door, reached inside and switched on the light. The glow from the lamp revealed the suitcase on a chair, open and half-filled with clothing.

"In there?" Helen asked, her face grim and her eyes strangely bright.

"—Yes. Yes, the letter is inside, hidden in the lining."

"Get it."

"First I must remove the clothes. As you can see, I have started to pack, and I—"

"Hurry and get it. I want to see it."

"Helen, I am just as anxious to show you the letter as you are to read it. However, I can't possibly get it out of its hiding place until you release my arm."

Vickie felt the gripping fingers relax and loosen a little, but with a hesitancy. Helen was uncertain, and her eyes had darkened with suspicion. Then, as though reluctantly, she freed the arm. "It had better be in there. You'll be sorry if you have lied to me," she warned. "More sorry than you can imagine."

"It's here," Vickie said. "Just be patient. I'll find it." She reached into the suitcase, lifted out her lingerie, her dresses, sweaters and shoes. Now her fingers felt the suit that was Phil's. The one he disliked. How heavy it seemed as she lifted it, and then with a sudden motion she flung it over the woman's head, shoved her backward and fled through the open door.

Now she was running back along the balcony and down the stairway, but in a moment she knew her attempt to escape had been futile. Helen was at her heels, her quick breaths seemed to be against Vickie's neck, and twice her fingers brushed at her hair. It was at the foot of the stairs that Vickie felt Helen's hands grab her shoulders, and she cried out with fear and pain.

"Helen! Please!"

"You lying, cheating little—"

"Let me go!" Vickie shouted. "You're hurting me!"

"Now I know who pushed Anita into the well," Helen cried. "It was you. You wanted Jim for yourself, didn't you? Oh, it's all so clear to me now. It was you! You!" the woman shrieked. "So this is how you shall join her in death. What better way? What better place?"

"No! Helen, no!"

Vickie, struggling, was being drawn toward it, nearer and nearer to where the bucket hung and the iron twisted into flowers and leaves above it. Black flowers over the well. A black wreath above her grave.

Then a sudden cry like that of an injured animal broke from Helen's throat. She stopped and stood motionless, frozen, rigid as a board. Her eyes were wide and glazed, and when Vickie followed that look of staring horror that was on the woman's face, she, too, stood as though impaled with a spear of terror and disbelief.

Beside the well stood a small transparent figure of a young woman. In the light from the moon, the silver-gold of her hair shimmered, and the misty blue of her garment seemed to melt into the soft night air around her. Here was a gossamer vision—but the face was clear, and it looked at them now. That same cameo-like countenance that had appeared to Vickie from the darkness of the well.

Kathleen!

11

VICKIE RAN. SHE could not quite remember Helen's tight grip leaving her shoulders, nor could she recall spanning the distance of the hallway. She knew she had thrown open the front door, and now she was running into the night, out through the open gates and on and on until she dropped exhausted behind a ledge of rock. She could go no farther. Her heart pounded, her pulses hammered against her temples and she was gasping for breath. For life.

After a long moment she leaned forward to look around the protecting ledge until she could see the house and the route she had taken from it. Nothing moved. Rays from the moon flooded the land with light, and she knew that Helen had not followed her. In all directions Vickie peered, ever cautious, ever wary. Where was the woman? Surely she would soon appear; surely she would make every attempt to locate this hiding place. Once she had recovered from the shock they had both experienced she would let nothing stand in her way to accomplish what she had to do.

Vickie shuddered and waited. For what seemed an eternity she waited, looking closely at every shadow, listening intently to every sound of the night. Helen, too, out there somewhere, must be watching and listening and hating with a heart frozen by terror. Vickie knew that if it had not been for this rock, Helen would be able to see her as clearly as they had seen—Kathleen; Kathleen whose image was still before Vickie's eyes. She would always see her, and how incredible that it had been this woman's disembodied spirit who had saved her from Helen's insane fury.

As the moments wore on, Vickie became conscious of pain. She could still feel Helen's fingers digging into the sides of her neck. She ran her hand along the back of her head, finding a lump, which had to be the result of Helen's striking her. How quickly it had all taken place! One moment she was fighting to release herself from the woman's grasp, and the next she was whirling through blazing colors into the blackness of the trunk.

Now she held her breath and listened. It seemed as if her heart had become a wild bird fluttering to break out of a cage, and she could not control the violent trembling of her entire body. She had heard something, hadn't she? Or was it an echo of screams and shouts and threats and pleading words? Might Helen be calling her, as she had done yesterday out there on the desert?

The night was silent. Vickie heard nothing now, and she leaned back against the rock and tried to control the turmoil surging within her body and mind. There was nothing left to do but wait and watch and listen. She did not know how much time passed before her body again tightened like a spring, and she was once more painfully alert—listening intently now, for there was a sound, the sound of a car some distance away. Its engine had been started, then had sputtered and finally roared. How clearly this noise had traveled to her over the desert! Could it be, she wondered, that Helen had reached her trailer, and . . . Yes! Yes, this would be quite possible and Vickie scanned the moon-bathed terrain. If Helen drove over the area, her headlights searching here and there! Oh, God!

Now Vickie rose to her knees, wondering if she should make a dash for the house? But then—what if the car she heard was not Helen's? The woman might still be in the house. She could easily visualize her going from one window to another looking out sharply, searchingly. Or perhaps she had run from the patio, out through the back gate and around the wall where she was now hiding and peering into the night. How cunningly she would wait for her victim to emerge from concealment!

Vickie sat down again in the soft sand and pressed her body against the rock. She would not return to the house. She could still hear the car, but the sound was diminishing, fading away quite rapidly. It might have been Helen. It might have been anyone. And Vickie bit her lip as she peered thoughtfully into the night. She pondered certain possibilities. Would this woman dare leave and not seek her out, Vickie wondered, after all she had learned? After all that had happened? She was beginning to doubt this and now her heart beat faster and faster making her wonder if her fate was to be death by fright.

With this thought a new determination was born within her. Now her heart drummed more from anger than fear, and her hand reached out and closed around a sharp stone. She could still fight, she told herself. She was not finished yet. She raised herself enough to look again at the house and saw no one. Her eyes followed the wall. No one. Not a shadow moved, and there were many. Some from Joshua trees appeared as tall figures with arms outstretched—but motionless—inert.

Again she leaned back and forced herself to relax. There was nothing left to do but wait and think. Her mind told her that Helen was not prowling around searching for her. The cry that had escaped from the woman's throat, when she had seen Kathleen's ghost, was a sound of such electrifying terror and horror, that only her own death would have prevented Helen from breaking away as fast as she could. Vickie could picture her now, driving like a wild thing through the night, putting as many miles between herself and this place as possible, the house Kathleen still occupied.

And with this thought, Vickie's eyes wandered to the star-filled inverted bowl of the heavens above her, and she let its dazzling beauty pour into her to wash away the doubts and fears and pain that had gripped her for so long, too long. They are like diamonds, she told herself, diamonds strewn on black velvet across the counter of a jewelry store. Sparkling.

It was a dreamy interlude lulling her with soothing richness and several moments passed before she became aware of something different, something obtrusive. Into her consciousness had come the realization of a foreign stab of light that should not have been, and her eyes peered now, not at the sky, but at the earth. How strange! Whatever it had been it was not visible now. There was nothing but moonlight and starlight across a scene as still as though it were a painting, a—she gasped. There it was again; an eerie light cutting across the landscape. And now it was gone.

Curious, alert and rigid, she watched closely, hardly daring to breathe; and after a tense moment she saw a flash of white. Signals? Might someone be signaling? Who? Why? What could it mean? And chilled, she pulled her sweater closer around her, crouched down and waited as an animal ready to spring. Ready to run.

Then she knew, across the desert came a sound of a car which made her gasp with a mixture of hope and fear. Might Norman be returning? Norman! She shivered. He could be dead. Telling Jim what he had learned might have been the final deadly mistake of his life. Perhaps it was Jim approaching. The car was drawing nearer and nearer, and now the light flashed closer and oftener. Jim was racing home, not wanting to reveal his location in case he was being pursued, yet not wanting to become lost. Even he shared this fear with others.

She shook her head. Surely these thoughts were mad. She must gather her wits and stop permitting her mind to fly off on a tangent wrought of wild fantasies. But then, there was a car coming, and . . . Vickie froze. Apparently it had made a sharp turn and for a fleeting instant it blinded her.

"Good God!" she cried out in horror, for now she knew it was Helen who was there. Helen in the camper. Helen was not going to let her live. She was coming for her, just as Vickie had first feared she might.

She ran. The rock that had shielded her was much too near the road, too near the house. How easily Helen would find her with the beams of light! Why had she not been running away all this time? She should have known. How illogical she had been. How foolishly she had wrapped herself in stars, luxuriating in their beauty. How pleasant! How easy! How fatal!

The car was coming fast. Its lights were here, there and sweeping the entire area around her as the vehicle deliberately was being driven from side to side.

Darting frantically, Vickie knew it was now she who was fleeing like a wild thing through the night from tree to tree, bush to bush, rock to rock. Of one thing she was sure. It was a fiend who searched for her, one who would never give up. The sound of the car's engine was now like the muffled roar of a strange fierce animal. And Vickie had to suppress her desire to scream again and again.

Twice she fell, and the last time had been a stroke of fortune, for the light had flashed above her as she lay prone upon the earth. She found that she still clutched the sharp stone in one hand, and now with the trembling fingers of her other hand she unbuttoned her sweater and stealthily pulled it over her head to conceal her vivid hair. She did not move, only her heart was running and her lungs were gulping in deep draughts of desert air.

The camper passed her hiding place, passed the house and went on along the narrow road, but she knew it would return. Fingering the stone she wondered. Would she use it? Could she kill? Even in self-defense would she take another's life? She realized she did not know the answer, not really. However, in her mind she felt herself pounding Helen's face with this stone, and hammering against her skull until she was no longer able to do so. And with horror and a violent shudder, she erased from her thoughts this sickening mental image.

Quickly she scrambled to her feet and again she was running from the searching light knowing that Helen would soon turn around and come back. Several times she winced with pain as her legs and arms were scratched and torn by the thorns that were everywhere, reaching for her, tormenting her. She cried silently in the darkness from the stinging lacerations and from her despair.

A dark mass loomed ahead of her in the distance, and she knew that here must be the hill she had climbed previously finding Helen's camper hidden on the other side. She scanned the area to her left where she had wandered before. She knew there had been rocks and massive boulders, for it had been from these that the sound of her name had seemed to be emanating eerily. Here was the only place, she decided, where she would have a chance of eluding her pursuer. An equal chance they would have in there, for Helen would have to leave her camper and travel on foot among the many rocks. It was toward these that Vickie made her way breathlessly, laboriously, but with the knowledge that here lay her only hope of survival. Once more this night, Vickie knew she must fight for her life, and she did not deceive herself. Unless help arrived, this was to be a struggle to the very end.

As she made her way on and on she looked back over her shoulder time and again. The headlight beams were growing nearer. Helen had turned around and was retracing her route. She would probably stop at the house to see if her quarry had returned to it. But wait—Vickie thought, as she reconsidered this possibility. No, she told herself. Never would the woman enter the Desert Flower again. Not now. Not with the presence that haunted it.

Vickie tried to hurry faster. She would have welcomed the extra time given to her if Helen had had the courage to search the house. And now she wondered if their thoughts were traveling the same channel. Once this woman could not locate her huddled behind cactus or smaller rocks of the desert, would her eyes turn also to the high sharp ridge ahead?

She shuddered.

Oh, God! she thought, I feel as though I were lost at night in mid-ocean. Lost, alone and terrified. I am in a small boat and the rays from the moon reveal mounds that are swells, and my enemy—a shark—a silvery white shark, its body gleaming in the moonlight knows that it has the advantage. Its surroundings are familiar to it. It is far larger and stronger and vicious. It is only a matter of time until its jaws open wide and . . .

It seemed an eternity before she reached the trail leading to the rocks—and the cemetery. And once she had, the feeling of being lost vanished. She knew where she was. How well she knew where she was! And now as she trudged along she stopped often to look back and suddenly she realized that she had not seen the lights for several minutes. Could it be that Helen had given up the search? Would it be possible that she would withdraw, leaving alive the only person who knew of her guilt? No, Vickie told herself. She must not again fall into the trap of underestimating the woman's grim determination and cunning.

Vickie looked at the sky. Had the moon ever been so bright? The desert lay silver and blue and lavender. Only the shadows were dark, dark purple and indigo. Helen could follow the road without lights. She could drive almost anywhere across this terrain without lights. She only needed them to seek out her victim.

Hesitantly Vickie paused and holding her breath she listened, for it seemed she had again heard that low, muffled roar of an engine. Yes! There it was! The sound was floating on the soft desert air, but how difficult it was to discern its direction! Only one thing was clear. The damnable vehicle was approaching quickly for the sound was growing louder and louder. Suddenly Vickie found herself bathed in light! Now as she screamed and ran, through the night came another sound. It was laughter; a ghastly, hideous laugh.

Vickie left the trail. She stumbled and fell over a rock. But here, in this maze of the earth's outcropping no wheels could follow her, and once again she was running. On and on she went, not daring to stop to look back. She darted behind the Joshuas, and every large thorn-bearing plant that rose before her—trying to put as many obstacles as possible between her and her pursuer and the cluster of boulders ahead. She would reach them, she knew, or die in the attempt.

She could hear nothing now except her own footsteps, her breathing and the pounding of her heart that seemed to be hammering against her eardrums. She was nearing the rocks. Thank God she was apparently going to reach them and their blessed shadows. With this realization a new surge of strength seemed to fill her. She moved faster now, and as the dark shadows enfolded her she knew that Helen could not see her. Surely she could not, yet—Vickie was aware of an eerie sensation that someone was watching her, and cautiously she slowed her pace and looked uncertainly at the large formation ahead.

What she had hoped was to be her sanctuary, her fortress, stood like an island surrounded by a sea of desert sand. If Helen had not followed her on foot, the same route Vickie had taken, then she had chosen another course, perhaps a shorter one, and was now in there, somewhere—waiting. Could this be, Vickie wondered? Or was the woman waiting, still in her camper; patient and watching and knowing that sooner or later her victim would have to emerge?

Quickly she glanced back. She could no longer see the car's headlights, only the glow of the moon was visible turning the trees into dark silhouettes. Vickie stood unmoving, listening. There were many sounds. The emptiness of the desert was an illusion. It was occupied by creatures of the night, and she could hear their small sounds now. The slip of running lizards, a scurrying that might have been a jackrabbit, a tiny squeak that could be that of a scuttling desert mouse.

But then her eyes widened. Something large had moved. No more than a shadow it had been, and now it was gone

Helen! It had to be Helen, and she had stepped behind a Joshua tree. Hidden.

Vickie ran toward the rocks as fast as she could, and as their walls enclosed her she searched in a frenzied kind of way for a hiding place; the darkest shadow, that cleft to the right, the large crevice ahead of her. Perhaps if she crouched down between the rocks to her left—or would it be wiser to keep running, making her way through this maze and out the other side and on to huddle behind the tombstones in the cemetery?

She knew she must make up her mind quickly for that moving shadow had not been far away. Obviously Helen had seen her, or she wouldn't have vanished like a wisp of blue behind the tree.

Vickie pressed her body tightly against the rocky wall and moved on silently. She must not trap herself, she was thinking. She mustn't lose sight of an exit. How easy it would be to step into a place from which she could not escape if Helen discovered her! Stealthily she inched her way toward the far side of her fortress. Every minute seemed an eternity.

Where was Helen?

Knowing she must have been seen, Vickie wondered if Helen would now take a different path into the nest of rocks, and she tried to peer into all directions at once, while the thought of moving right into the mad woman's reach turned her to ice.

She listened.

Somewhere there had been a shrill animal sound followed by silence—a deadly silence. If she could only hear the footsteps that neared her! If she could only again see a wavering shadow. It was not knowing that was tearing her apart.

The shadows cast from the rocks were all around her, and she studied them closely. Then suddenly she gasped.

There had been a movement that had caught her eye. It was not far away. Atop a nearby rock, nearly four feet high, something had curled, entwining itself. A shadow of Helen's fingers? Her arm?

Now Vickie clamped her hand across her lips to stop the scream that nearly escaped. The shadow had become a sinuous thing, writhing and undulating! A snake! And before Vickie's fascinated stare it coiled, its body now visible in the moonlight.

Instinctively she moved away from the rock at her back and cringed. Then what happened next took place so swiftly that it seemed to all be a simultaneous action. Helen was there, a dark form against the light behind her. There was a dry, crackling rattle, and—

"Helen!" Vickie screamed. "Look out!"

The snake struck with rapier speed. Its darting head had been too fast for Vickie's eyes to see. All that appeared to her now was Helen's hand grabbing the side of her throat. And then came the scream that seemed to echo throughout the rocks and across the desert, filling the night. Suddenly, Helen turned and stumbled into the darkness.

Helen shouldn't run, Vickie was thinking as she scrambled over the rocks, making her way as quickly as possible out of this place which she had struggled so desperately to reach. She should not run. She should stay as quiet as possible. And then with the ridge behind her, Vickie saw something else. The camper.

But where was Helen? Surely she had tried to reach it. Might she be inside? Vickie hurried toward the vehicle. She must help her if possible. The thought of the snake and what had taken place made her tremble uncontrollably. Helen being struck—perhaps in the throat . . . Vickie gasped and hurried forward.

There was not a sound coming from the vicinity of the camper. There was no one on the seat. When Vickie ran around to the door, she found it locked with no light coming from within. Now she hurried to the cab to see if the key was in the ignition. It wasn't. Helen was not here. She was out there—somewhere—alone with death as her grim penalty.

12

VICKIE FLICKED ON the headlights of the camper hoping someone would see and come to investigate. Norman or Jim or a patrolman, perhaps. She debated waiting in the shadows, but the thought of the snake caused her to change her mind. To remain in the cab of the camper would be best. From here she could watch. From here she had a wide view of the area where Helen had vanished.

As she waited, all that had happened to her since Friday night unreeled in her mind. The bewilderment, the terror, the freezing horror of the experience. But after a while she meditated on the results. She had learned some surprising things. Kathleen was not the only one who possessed a well. She, too, had one, she realized, one from which she could draw strength that she never knew she had. Suddenly she felt more independent, and self-reliant. She could cope with the blows dealt to her. And she knew something else. There was more to life and death then she had ever truly imagined. There was more than she could understand.

Time passed. Had it been one hour or more? No matter. Two beams of light were now approaching rapidly along the trail, and Vickie stepped out of the camper. Who was racing toward her, Norman or Jim? If it were neither, if it should be a patrolman again, the same one who had found her before . . . She hoped not. How difficult it would be to explain it all to him!

Now the car, in a cloud of dust, came to a halt, and a tall slim man jumped from it. "Vickie!" he shouted.

"Norman! Oh, Norman!"

"Vickie." She could see in the moonlight the deep concern in his eyes and his voice had been a caress. "Vickie, are you all right? What happened? What are you doing here? Jim and I came home and found the front door wide open and you and Helen gone. Where is she?"

"Out there," she said, nodding toward the area to her left. "She was bitten by a rattlesnake, bitten on the side of the neck and she ran."

"Good Lord! We must find her."

"Norman, she can't be alive. Not now. Not after this length of time. Not after what happened. And there is something else I must tell you. She is the one responsible for your sister's death, and indirectly for that of her own daughter."

He was staring at her, and now in the distance another set of lights could be seen.

"Someone is coming," she said. And after a long moment he nodded.

"It's Jim. He waited to call the highway patrol. Get into

my car, Vickie. I'll help him look for Helen until the patrolmen arrive and then I'll take you back to the house."

Jim looked at her quizzically, then at the camper and at
Norman. At Norman's insistence he hurried off with him,
asking questions, shaking his head in disbelief and soon
the two men became shadows wandering, weaving their
way across the desert until they disappeared into the wil-
derness.

From far away came the sound of a siren, and again she
thought of Anita. First the wailing had been for her. Now it
was for her mother. It became louder and louder. What a
chilling sound this was, always denoting trouble and sadness for someone. And when Vickie watched the oncoming
car's spotlight sweep across the desert, she was thankful
that Helen had not had one of these. If she had . . . Vickie
rubbed her hands along her arms and breathed deeply.
But she didn't have one, she told herself. And I am here
and alive and —and I want to go home. I want to look over
the bay again, and walk in the morning fog, and stand
atop Nob Hill at night while the wind blows through my
hair and the city is spread out below like a carpet of
jewels.

Soon she was talking to the patrolmen, and with their
flashlights they, too, joined the search. Before long Norman
returned and together they drove back to the house.

"We didn't find her, but they will," he said. "And Jim
will help. I now know that it wasn't he who . . . Tonight
on our way back from Palm Springs I told him everything
I had learned and I accused him of leaving Kathleen to
die. He convinced me my accusations were unfounded.
But tell me, Vickie. What took place here? Why were you
and Helen out there, and what about the camper?"

She shook her head. "I don't want to go over all that, not
now. I'll tell you tomorrow. Norman, Phil didn't come back
with you, did he."

"No, Vickie."

She nodded. "Helen told me that he and Jim had formed a plan—one to have me lost in the desert."

"I know."

"That was what you had suspected, wasn't it?"

"Well, I—I wasn't really sure what was going on. I only knew you were in danger. Tonight Jim poured out the whole story to me, Vickie. It seems there had been a sordid scandal during their university years and Jim was deeply involved. Phil and Jim were close friends in those days, fraternity brothers, and it was Phil who extricated him by lying and furnishing Jim with an alibi. And then it was Phil who, during this last year, renewed their acquaintance for a reason. He wanted the favor repaid."

"Then it was a kind of blackmail," she said, and he nodded.

"He needed Jim's help in a plan," Norman told her, "to which Jim reluctantly agreed."

"Yes? And then what?" she asked, for he had fallen silent.

"Are you sure you want to hear all this?" he asked. "I mean—shouldn't we wait?"

"No. I must hear it now. Go on."

"Well, under the pretense of negotiating a sale, your husband was to come here and bring you with him. Then he and Jim were to go to Palm Springs, but leave Phil's car along the road where it would be found, of course, and a search would follow. Phil was to do just what he did, buy a ticket at the airport under an assumed name and leave. And Jim . . . "

"Tell me," she said.

"Jim was to do what I suspected he had done to Kathleen; take you out on the desert and leave you. The assumption would have been that you had wandered off and became lost while looking for your husband."

And I did that, Vickie was thinking. That is exactly what I did.

"There was to be a delay in the realization that you were missing," Norman was saying. "A long delay—too long."

Vickie looked at him. "Helen said that Jim did not intend to go through with this part of the plan," she told him, while thinking of how right the woman was when she had said that nothing happened here that she did not know about.

"He didn't. I now know that Jim is incapable of murder," Norman told her.

"But Phil is," Vickie murmured.

"Vickie, that chapter of your life is closed. You must forget about him."

"He wanted to be a widower," she said thoughtfully, and felt only a numbness inside herself. "For some reason this would simplify things for him. I—I don't understand why."

Norman did not answer her, and his very silence told her that he knew the answer. "Norman, why?"

"There's the house ahead, Vickie."

"Norman! Why?"

"Okay, Vickie. You had an insurance policy, didn't you?" He shuddered. "I mean, you *have* an insurance policy, haven't you? He took out a large one on your life, it seems."

She gasped. "But — Norman! You mean—money? He wanted me dead for the money?"

He nodded. "And according to what he told Jim, your decorator shop—the business—the antiques would bring a nice price when sold. Your husband is your sole heir. Right?"

"Yes. But not for long. He is soon to be my ex-husband. Norman, where is he now?"

"Well, he's not in San Francisco. He's left the country. And Vickie, he isn't alone. The woman with him is—a rather wealthy one, it seems."

"Phil," she said thoughtfully, "the ambitious one. Yes, yes. This would be Phil."

"I'm sorry, Vickie."

"Thank you, but don't be. Somehow I'm glad it's over. The marriage wasn't any good. I married a man who never really existed. He was only an image I had created from wishes and longing and imagination. I wanted him to be someone he was not and never could become. I made a mistake, one that nearly cost me my life. Never marry a stranger."

"Vickie, I want to see you away from all this. Will you let me visit you in San Francisco when you get back?" Norman asked.

"I was hoping you'd ask," Vickie answered with a smile.